The REAL High School Survival Guide

Kevin Lawson

Published by Michael Pollick, 2024.

THE REAL HIGH SCHOOL SURVIVAL GUIDE

First edition. August 26, 2024.

Copyright © 2024 Kevin Lawson.

ISBN: 979-8227813329

Written by Kevin Lawson.

Table of Contents

The REAL High School Survival Guide

Kevin Lawson

Welcome To The High School Jungle

It's the first day of school, and I'm standing in front of this colossal high school, which looks more like a small college campus than a place where I'm supposed to learn about algebra and Shakespeare. Seriously, this place is so big that I half expect to see a tour guide waving a flag, leading a group of lost freshmen around like we're all on some kind of educational safari. "And over here, you'll see the cafeteria, where the mystery meat is served with a side of regret!"

So, there I am, clutching my schedule like it's a life raft in a sea of chaos. I mean, who needs a GPS when you have a school map that looks like it was designed by a mad scientist? I'm pretty sure I saw a "You Are Here" dot that was just a suggestion, like, "Good luck finding your first-period class, buddy!" I squint at the map, trying to decipher the hieroglyphics that are the building numbers, and I can't help but wonder if I should have brought a compass, a snack, and maybe a Sherpa.

I finally muster the courage to step inside, and the first thing that hits me is the sound—oh my goodness, the sound! It's a cacophony of laughter, shouting, and the unmistakable sound of lockers slamming shut like the world's most chaotic percussion section. I feel like I've walked into the middle of a high school musical, but instead of singing, everyone is just yelling about who has the latest TikTok dance down. I'm standing there, half-expecting someone to break into song about the joys of geometry, but instead, I get a front-row seat to the drama of teenage life.

Navigating the hallways is like trying to swim upstream in a river of hormones and backpacks. I'm dodging kids left and right, like I'm in some sort of bizarre game of Frogger. I spot a girl who looks like she's auditioning for the role of Queen Bee, surrounded by her entourage, and I think, "Great, I've just entered the Hunger Games of high school social dynamics." I can practically hear the dramatic music playing in the background as I try to blend in, hoping to avoid any eye contact that might lead to an awkward interaction.

I finally find my first class, and as I walk in, I feel like I'm entering a gladiator arena. The teacher is this no-nonsense type who looks like she could bench press a car and has a glare that could melt steel. She introduces herself and immediately starts calling roll, and I'm praying my name doesn't sound too weird. "Here!" I say, and it comes out like a squeak. I internally cringe. I can feel the eyes of my classmates on me, judging my existence like I'm the new kid in a sitcom. I half expect someone to shout, "You're not in the right show!"

After surviving that class, I make my way to lunch, which is a whole other adventure. The cafeteria is a sprawling expanse of tables, and I feel like I'm trying to find a seat at a concert. I scan the room, looking for a friendly face, but all I see are cliques that seem to have been formed in the primordial ooze of middle school. I finally spot an empty seat at a table, and I approach it like it's a throne, hoping the occupants won't throw me out like some unwanted jester.

I sit down, and the conversation around me is a mix of gossip, memes, and the most intense debate I've ever witnessed over which pizza place has the best crust. I try to contribute, but all I can think about is how I just survived my first day in this colossal jungle of high school. I realize that everyone else is just as lost and confused as I am, and maybe, just maybe, we'll all figure this out together. Or at least find the best pizza place before the year ends.

https://app.videogen.io/view/igyuoa

Another One Rides The Bus

You know, there's something uniquely chaotic about riding the bus to high school that no one ever really talks about. It's like a rite of passage, but instead of a warm embrace, you get a cold slap in the face from reality. Let me paint you a picture. You wake up at the crack of dawn, and by that I mean the sun is still debating whether or not to rise. You stumble out of bed, hair looking like you just survived a tornado, and you throw on whatever clothes you can find, which, if we're being honest, is probably a mismatched outfit that your future self will definitely judge you for. But hey, it's high school. You're not there to win a fashion award, right?

You rush through breakfast, which for me was usually a granola bar I'd shove in my pocket as I sprinted out the door. Because, of course, I'm going to need the energy to deal with the human zoo that is the school bus. The bus stop is like a scene from a wildlife documentary. You've got the jocks, who are basically lions, strutting around, flexing their muscles, and making sure everyone knows they're the kings of the jungle. Then there are the goth kids, lurking in the shadows like mysterious wolves, sharing deep, dark secrets about their favorite bands. And let's not forget the band geeks, who are like the diligent little beavers, always working hard, but somehow still managing to create chaos with their instruments.

When the bus finally arrives, it's like the gates of a chaotic amusement park opening up. Everyone rushes in, and you have to dodge backpacks like they're ninja stars. You can't just stroll onto the bus; you have to fight your way in, elbowing your way through a crowd of teenagers who have suddenly forgotten what basic manners are. You find a seat, and if you're lucky, it's not next to someone who smells like they bathed in a cologne factory explosion.

Now, let's talk about the seating arrangements. You've got the front seats, where the "good kids" sit, pretending to be focused on their homework while secretly eavesdropping on the drama unfolding in the back. The middle seats are the wild card zone—somewhere between the cool kids and the kids who are just trying to survive the day. And then there are the back seats, the legendary realm of chaos where anything goes. This is where the laughter erupts, where the inside jokes fly faster than the bus itself, and where you might just witness a spontaneous karaoke session to the latest pop hit.

But let's not forget the bus driver, the unsung hero of this whole operation. The bus driver is like a reluctant referee in a wrestling match, trying to maintain some semblance of order while the kids are plotting the next great rebellion. You can always tell when they've had enough—there's that moment when they slam on the brakes a little too hard, and you can feel the panic ripple through the bus. Suddenly, everyone's silent, like they've just been caught doing something they shouldn't.

And then there's the ride itself. It's a rollercoaster of emotions. One moment you're laughing so hard you're almost crying because someone made a joke about the math teacher's questionable fashion choices, and the next you're dealing with the existential crisis of realizing you forgot to do your homework. You try to distract yourself by staring out the window, watching the world zoom by, but all you can think about is how you're probably going to fail that algebra test.

Finally, you arrive at school, and as you step off the bus, you're greeted by the chaos of the high school parking lot. It's like emerging from a war zone, and you can't help but feel a mix of relief and dread. You've survived another bus ride, another day of navigating the wild world of high school. But deep down, you know you'll miss those chaotic mornings, the laughter, the friendships, and yes, even the smell of the bus. Because in the end, those moments are what make the journey worthwhile.

https://app.videogen.io/view/sbhqaz

The Peter Brady Singers

You know, when I signed up for high school choir, I thought I was making a bold move. I imagined myself standing in front of a crowd, belting out show tunes, my voice soaring like a majestic eagle. I pictured the applause, the accolades, the adoring fans. What I didn't anticipate was that my journey into the world of choral music would resemble more of a slapstick comedy than a Broadway musical.

Let me take you back to my first day of choir practice. I walked into the music room, all bright-eyed and bushy-tailed, ready to conquer the world of harmonies. I was greeted by a sea of faces, some of whom looked like they had just come from a vocal masterclass, while I was still trying to figure out how to hit a note without sounding like a dying cat. There was this one girl, Sarah, who I swear could hit notes that were not even on the piano. I stood next to her, and suddenly I felt like a kazoo in a symphony orchestra.

The choir director, Mr. Thompson, was a man with the energy of a caffeinated squirrel. He clapped his hands and announced, "Welcome to choir! Let's start with warm-ups!" Warm-ups? I thought we were just going to sing. Apparently, warm-ups involved a series of vocal exercises that sounded suspiciously like a game of animal impressions. "Let's do a siren!" he shouted, and suddenly we were all wailing like we were auditioning for a role in a horror movie. I was trying to sound like a police siren, but it came out more like a cat who just discovered the vacuum cleaner.

Then came the scales. Oh, the scales. I had no idea that singing could be so mathematical. "Do, re, mi, fa, so, la, ti, do!" Mr. Thompson bellowed, and we all echoed back like a bunch of confused parrots. I was convinced I was going to end up in a musical version of "Survivor," where the last person standing would win a record deal. But instead, I was just trying to remember which note came after "ti," while simultaneously trying not to trip over my own feet.

As the weeks went by, I began to realize that choir was not just about singing. It was about teamwork, camaraderie, and a surprising amount of drama. There was the rivalry between the sopranos and altos that could rival any reality TV show. The sopranos were convinced they were the stars of the show, while the altos were plotting their comeback with some fierce harmonies. I found myself in the middle, trying to mediate like a peacekeeper at a family reunion. "Can't we all just get along?" I would plead, only to be met with glares that could freeze lava.

And then there was the annual choir concert. The moment we had all been waiting for, where we would showcase our hard work and dedication. I envisioned myself standing under the spotlight, a vision of grace and poise. Instead, I found myself backstage, frantically trying to remember the lyrics to a song I had learned two weeks prior. My mind went blank, and I could only remember the chorus, which I had accidentally mixed up with the lyrics to a Taylor Swift song. So there I was, singing about heartbreak while my choir mates were harmonizing about friendship. I'm pretty sure the audience was just as confused as I was.

But you know what? Despite the chaos, the missed notes, and the occasional wardrobe malfunction, I wouldn't trade my time in choir for anything. I learned that it's okay to be a little off-key sometimes, that laughter can be the best harmony, and that the real magic happens when you embrace the absurdity of it all. So here's to high school choir, where every note is an adventure, and every practice is a chance to find joy in the music—no matter how hilariously out of tune we might be.

https://app.videogen.io/view/udpwbe

High School Marching Band Orders

You know, when I think back to my high school days, the first thing that comes to mind is marching band. Not because it was the highlight of my teenage years, but rather because it was a series of unfortunate events wrapped in a shiny uniform. Seriously, if you want to know what it's like to be in a marching band, just imagine a group of people who can't walk and chew gum at the same time, all trying to play an instrument while marching in formation. It's like herding cats, but the cats are wearing polyester and trying to remember which way is left.

Let's talk about the uniforms for a second. Whoever designed those things must have been a sadist. They were hot, itchy, and about as flattering as a potato sack. I mean, who thought it was a good idea to put a hundred teenagers in shiny, tight-fitting pants that could double as a sauna? The hats! Oh, the hats! They were these giant, feathered monstrosities that made us look like we were auditioning for a role in a bad historical reenactment. And don't even get me started on the gloves. White gloves. In a marching band. Who decided that was a good idea? By the end of the first rehearsal, those gloves were so stained that you'd think we were performing in a barbecue joint rather than a football game.

And the music! Oh, the music! I still have nightmares about the endless hours spent practicing the same three notes over and over again. We had this one song that was supposed to be a rousing fight song, but it ended up sounding like a cat being strangled. I mean, how hard is it to play a G, C, and D chord? Apparently, very hard. I played the trumpet, and let me tell you, there's nothing more humiliating than being the only one who can't hit the high note in "Louie Louie." You could hear my squeak echoing through the stadium like an air horn gone wrong.

Then there were the formations. Marching band is basically a high-stakes game of human Tetris. You have to memorize where you're supposed to stand, which way you're supposed to turn, and how to avoid stepping on the person next to you while simultaneously not tripping over your own feet. I once got so caught up in trying to remember my spot that I ended up marching right into the tuba section. Let me tell you, nothing says "I'm a graceful musician" quite like getting tackled by a tuba.

And the parades! Oh, the parades! I thought they would be glamorous—like the Rose Parade or something. But no, it was more like walking a mile in the scorching sun, surrounded by people who clearly had no idea what a marching band was supposed to look like. There I was, trying to look dignified while sweating like a pig in a sauna, and all I could hear were the parents yelling, "Look, honey! There's our band!" as if we were some kind of circus act. I half expected a clown to pop out of the drumline and start juggling.

Then there were the competitions. You haven't truly experienced anxiety until you're standing on a field, waiting for the judges to critique your every move. It's like being on a first date where you know your date is judging your every flaw. You could hear a pin drop as we waited for the scores, and when we finally got them, it was like opening a bad report card. "Congratulations! You've managed to come in fourth place out of five bands!"

But despite all the sweat, the tears, and the questionable fashion choices, there was something magical about those moments. The camaraderie, the inside jokes, the shared misery—it was all part of the experience. We were a family, albeit a dysfunctional one, and those memories? They're worth their weight in gold. So here's to the awkward high school years, the marching band misadventures, and the friends who made it all worth it. Because at the end of the day, we may not have been the best band, but we sure knew how to have a good time.

https://app.videogen.io/view/qxzyie

Class Schedule A-GoGo

Choosing a class schedule in high school is like trying to solve a Rubik's Cube while riding a unicycle on a tightrope over a pit of alligators. It's an exercise in decision-making that can leave even the most seasoned veteran feeling like they've just emerged from a long, dark tunnel of confusion, clutching a schedule that feels more like a ransom note than a roadmap to academic success. You sit there, staring at the course catalog, and suddenly you're hit with a wave of existential dread. Do I really want to take AP Calculus, or should I just embrace my inner artist and sign up for Advanced Basket Weaving?

Let's face it: high school is the only place where you can simultaneously be an overachiever and a slacker, and the class schedule is the ultimate battleground of this internal conflict. On one hand, you have the "college prep" classes, which promise to prepare you for the rigorous academic life ahead. On the other hand, you have classes like "Intro to Video Game Design," which sounds like a delightful way to spend an hour pretending you're learning something while really just figuring out how to make Mario jump higher.

So, there you are, armed with a pencil and a sense of impending doom, trying to balance your interests with the expectations of your parents, teachers, and that one overly enthusiastic guidance counselor who seems to think you're destined to become the next Einstein. "You should really consider taking AP Chemistry," they say, as if you haven't already failed to distinguish between hydrogen and helium during a particularly traumatic fifth-grade science fair. Meanwhile, your best friend is trying to convince you to take "Creative Writing," because apparently, writing about your feelings is going to be the key to your future success. I mean, sure, if you want to major in "How to Cry on Command," then by all means, go for it.

Then there's the issue of electives. Oh, the glorious electives! They're like the dessert menu of your academic life. You can choose between "The Art of the Sandwich" and "Philosophy of the Selfie." But let's be real: how do you justify to your parents that you're spending an entire semester learning how to construct the perfect peanut butter and jelly? "Mom, it's not just a sandwich; it's an exploration of culinary identity!" Meanwhile, your parents are still trying to wrap their heads around why you think "Underwater Basket Weaving" is a legitimate career path.

And just when you think you've got it all figured out, you realize that your schedule is a jigsaw puzzle with missing pieces. You've got AP Physics and French IV stacked on top of each other, and the only thing you can say in French is "Je ne sais pas," which translates to "I don't know." Perfect! That's exactly how I feel about my life choices right now.

Then there's the infamous lunch period. You've got to strategically plan your classes around it because, let's be honest, lunch is the highlight of the day. You can't have a schedule that forces you to eat at 10:30 in the morning. What am I, a toddler? No, I want to eat when the sun is at its zenith, basking in the glory of cafeteria pizza that's definitely not made from real cheese.

Finally, after hours of deliberation, you submit your schedule, and the weight of the world is lifted off your shoulders. Only to realize that you've somehow signed up for "Advanced Knitting" instead of "AP History." But hey, at least I'll have a cozy sweater by the end of the semester. And isn't that what high school is really about? Learning to navigate the chaos, embracing the absurdity, and maybe, just maybe, finding a way to laugh through it all.

https://app.videogen.io/view/trkorj

The Entire Year In A Single Book

You know, when I first joined the high school yearbook staff, I thought I was signing up for something glamorous, like being a part of a secret society of creative geniuses. I imagined us sipping artisanal coffee, brainstorming brilliant ideas, and capturing the essence of our school in a way that would make even the most mundane moments feel like Oscar-winning moments. Instead, I found myself knee-deep in glitter, surrounded by a group of people who seemed to think that "teamwork" meant arguing over the best way to photograph a lunch lady.

Let me tell you, the first meeting was a revelation. Our faculty advisor, who clearly had a PhD in sarcasm, kicked things off by saying, "Welcome to the yearbook staff, where dreams go to die." I thought she was joking, but then she handed us a stack of forms that looked like they were compiled during the Stone Age. I mean, who knew that taking a picture of the varsity soccer team required a permission slip signed by every single player's great-grandmother? Seriously, I was half-expecting to have to send a carrier pigeon to get the necessary approvals.

And then there was the issue of the photo shoots. Apparently, capturing the essence of high school is best done in the most awkward poses imaginable. "Okay, everyone, let's do a jumping shot!" our photographer yelled, as if we were about to launch into a synchronized Olympic routine. So there we were, a bunch of teenagers who could barely coordinate our outfits, attempting to jump in unison while looking like we were auditioning for a role in a bad music video. Spoiler alert: we weren't. The only thing we managed to capture was the moment when Kevin, who was always a little too enthusiastic, landed face-first into a mud puddle. That photo ended up being the highlight of the "oops" page, and let me tell you, it took a solid week for him to recover from the embarrassment.

And how could I forget the endless debates over the theme? Oh, the theme! We threw around ideas like "A Year in Review" and "Memories in the Making," but somehow we always ended up back at "Let's Just Use Glitter and Call It a Day." It was like we were in a cult where the only requirement for membership was an unhealthy obsession with shiny things. I mean, at one point, I suggested "Under the Sea," and suddenly we were discussing how to incorporate mermaid tails into our photos. I'm still not sure how we went from high school to a Disney movie, but there we were, planning a photo shoot that involved inflatable dolphins and a kiddie pool.

Then came the writing part. You'd think it would be easy to sum up a year of high school in a few paragraphs, but somehow, it felt like trying to write the next great American novel. "Can we just say everyone had a great time?" I suggested, only to be met with glares that could probably melt steel. Apparently, "great time" wasn't going to cut it. So instead, we spent hours crafting sentences that were so flowery they could've been mistaken for a Shakespearean sonnet. "And thus, the Class of 2023 emerged from the chrysalis of adolescence, ready to take on the world!" I mean, come on, we're not writing a graduation speech; we're just trying to recap a year where half of us couldn't even remember our locker combinations.

By the time we were done, I was convinced that I had aged ten years. But you know what? As much as I complained, I wouldn't trade those chaotic moments for anything. We laughed, we cried (mostly from laughter), and we somehow managed to create something that captured the spirit of our school, even if it was sprinkled with a little too much glitter. So here's to the yearbook staff, the unsung heroes of high school memories, forever immortalized in pages filled with awkward poses, questionable themes, and a whole lot of glitter.

https://app.videogen.io/view/vmeubp

Hard-Hitting High School Journalism

I remember the first day I joined the high school newspaper staff, a day that promised excitement and adventure but ultimately delivered a hefty dose of reality. I walked in with dreams of being the next Woodward and Bernstein, ready to uncover the truth about cafeteria food quality and the mysterious disappearance of the gym's basketball. Instead, I was greeted by a room full of caffeine-fueled teenagers, hunched over laptops like they were trying to decode the secrets of the universe. Spoiler alert: they weren't. They were just trying to figure out how to make the headline "Seniors Win at Prom" sound more exciting than it actually was.

My first assignment was to cover the student council meeting. I approached it like I was walking into a high-stakes negotiation, armed with a notepad and a pen that was more interested in leaking ink than taking notes. I sat down, ready to capture every riveting moment of the council's discussions about the spring dance theme. Turns out, "Under the Sea" and "A Night in Paris" were the hottest topics of the day, and I was about to witness a full-blown debate about the merits of mermaids versus the Eiffel Tower. Who knew high school politics could be so... aquatic?

As I scribbled down quotes like "I just think we should go with something that really represents our school spirit, like 'Under the Sea,'" I realized that I was not only taking notes but also taking mental notes on how to survive this madness. I quickly learned that the key was to nod along, make occasional eye contact, and pray nobody asked me to weigh in. I mean, my expertise in high school dance themes was about as deep as a kiddie pool.

Then there was the time we decided to run a feature on the cafeteria staff. I thought it would be a lighthearted piece, maybe some fun facts about the lunch ladies and their secret chili recipe. Instead, I found myself knee-deep in a world of culinary chaos. One lady, Mrs. Thompson, revealed that the mystery meat was actually a blend of leftover whatever they could find in the freezer. I felt like I had stumbled upon a government conspiracy. I had to suppress my gag reflex while she passionately defended her "creative" cooking methods, and I found myself thinking that perhaps a little ignorance was bliss when it came to school lunches.

Of course, there were the moments of glory too. Like the time we covered the pep rally. I thought I'd get some great action shots of the cheerleaders flipping through the air, but what I ended up with was a series of blurry photos that looked like they were taken during an earthquake. Honestly, I think I captured more of the crowd's confused faces than the actual cheerleaders. My editor, who had a penchant for sarcasm, said they were "artistic interpretations of school spirit." I just called it a day and went for pizza instead.

And let's not forget the infamous "investigative piece" we did on the school's dress code. Now, that was a real can of worms. We interviewed students who had been sent home for wearing "inappropriate" clothing, and let me tell you, the stories were outrageous. One girl claimed her spaghetti strap was a "fashion statement" and not an affront to decency. I had to remind myself that these were high schoolers, not seasoned fashion critics. I mean, I once wore socks with sandals, and I'm still recovering from that fashion faux pas.

By the end of the year, I had learned a lot. I learned that the high school newspaper isn't just about reporting the news; it's about surviving the chaos, navigating the absurdity, and laughing through the ridiculousness of it all. I may not have uncovered any scandals or made headlines, but I did manage to survive a year filled with questionable cafeteria food, dramatic council meetings, and fashion debates that would make even the most seasoned journalists chuckle. And honestly, isn't that what high school is really about?

https://app.videogen.io/view/uvrjad

The Audio-Visual Squad: Waiting For The Beep

You know, when you think about high school jobs, you might picture kids flipping burgers or folding sweaters at the local mall. But me? I found my calling in the illustrious realm of the audio-visual department. Yes, the AV squad. The unsung heroes of the high school experience, the ones who get to play with all the fancy gadgets while the rest of the school is busy trying to figure out how to open a locker without a manual.

Let me tell you, the AV room was basically a glorified storage closet, but to me, it was a treasure trove. There was a certain thrill in the air every time I walked in, dodging the cobwebs and the occasional rogue mouse. I mean, who wouldn't want to spend their afternoons surrounded by old projectors that looked like they belonged in a museum? They were the kind of projectors that had probably been used to screen the first moon landing. I half expected Neil Armstrong to pop out and remind me to "one small step for man" my way out of there.

And then there were the microphones. Oh, the microphones! They were like the divas of the AV department. You'd think they were auditioning for a Broadway show with the way they malfunctioned at the most inopportune moments. "Can you hear me now?" became a mantra. I swear, every time we tried to set up for a school assembly, it was like a game of Russian roulette. One minute, you're confidently testing the mic, and the next, it's shrieking like a banshee. I've never seen teachers move so fast. You'd think I was conducting a fire drill instead of a sound check.

And let's not forget the glorious task of setting up for the annual talent show. I was the proud owner of a clipboard and a walkie-talkie, which, let me tell you, made me feel like I was in charge of the entire operation. "This is AV 101, over," I'd say, trying to sound all official while simultaneously trying to untangle a mess of cords that looked like it had been through a blender. I mean, how is it possible that every year, the cords multiplied? I half expected to find a family of mice living in there, plotting their escape.

The talent show itself was a spectacle. You had everything from the kid who could juggle flaming torches to the girl who sang like she was auditioning for American Idol. And then there was the band. Oh, the band. They were like a high school version of the Avengers, each member with their own unique superpower, but when they came together, it was like watching a train wreck in slow motion. I'd be standing at the soundboard, desperately trying to adjust the levels while simultaneously suppressing the urge to laugh. You haven't lived until you've heard a guitar solo that sounded like a cat being stepped on.

And the aftermath! After the show, the AV room looked like a tornado had hit it. Cables everywhere, empty soda cans littering the floor, and the faint smell of burnt popcorn wafting through the air. I'd spend hours cleaning up, wondering if I was running an AV department or a crime scene. I could hear the school janitor chuckling as he passed by, probably thinking I was one step away from declaring myself the King of the AV Jungle.

But you know what? I wouldn't trade it for anything. The camaraderie, the chaos, the sheer unpredictability of it all—it was the perfect blend of chaos and creativity. Sure, I didn't get the glory of the football team or the accolades of the honor roll, but I did get to be the wizard behind the curtain, pulling the strings and making sure the show went on. And honestly, there's a certain magic in that. So here's to the AV department, the unsung heroes of high school, where every day was an adventure and every mic check was a chance to shine—if only we could get the mic to work!

https://app.videogen.io/view/msrlbt

was an adventure and every mic check was a chance to shine—if only we could get the mic to work!

Driver's Education Class: A Study In Blood Pressure

I remember the day I walked into my high school driver education class, a room filled with a mix of excitement and dread, like a bag of gummy bears that had somehow been left in the sun too long. There we were, a group of teenagers, all convinced we were the next Vin Diesel, ready to conquer the roads with all the finesse of a seasoned stunt driver. Little did we know, we were more likely to resemble a herd of confused sheep, each of us trying to figure out how to parallel park without causing a minor international incident.

The first day was an introduction, which, in retrospect, felt more like a TED Talk on the dangers of texting while driving. Our instructor, Mr. Thompson, was a retired police officer with a mustache that could only be described as a small animal living on his upper lip. He had the kind of voice that could put a caffeinated squirrel to sleep, but he meant business. He started off with a story about a kid who thought he could impress his friends by doing donuts in a parking lot. Spoiler alert: the car didn't just spin, it ended up in a tree. Lesson learned: trees don't make good friends, and neither do insurance companies.

As we spent the next few weeks in the classroom, we were bombarded with rules and regulations that felt like they were written by a committee of overly cautious grandmothers. "Ten and two!" "Check your blind spots!" "Don't forget to signal!" I mean, who knew driving came with so many rules? It felt like preparing for an exam in an obscure subject, like Advanced Underwater Basket Weaving. I was convinced that I'd need a cheat sheet just to remember how to turn on the windshield wipers.

Finally, the day arrived for our first driving lesson. I climbed into the car with my classmate, Sarah, who had been practicing her "I'm totally calm and not terrified" face in the mirror for the last hour. We were paired with Mr. Thompson, who was now our personal driving coach. He strapped himself into the passenger seat like he was about to embark on a roller coaster ride, and honestly, it kind of felt that way. I gripped the steering wheel like it was the last lifeboat on the Titanic, and with a shaky breath, I turned the key in the ignition.

The car roared to life, and I could almost hear the engine laughing at my nervousness. As I pulled out of the parking lot, I felt like I was on a game show where the prize was not crashing. I was doing okay until I hit the first stop sign. Panic set in. Was I supposed to actually stop? I mean, I thought it was more of a suggestion? Clearly, Mr. Thompson didn't think so. "STOP!" he yelled, and I slammed on the brakes like I was trying to halt a runaway train. The car jolted, and Sarah let out a little squeak that sounded suspiciously like a mouse caught in a trap.

After a couple more near-death experiences involving curbs and pedestrians who clearly had no idea they were living dangerously, we finally made it back to the parking lot. I was sweating like I had just run a marathon, and Sarah looked like she had just survived a horror movie. "You did great!" she said, which I took as the world's most generous understatement. I was pretty sure I had left a trail of chaos in my wake.

The rest of the lessons followed a similar pattern of terror and triumph. I learned how to parallel park, which felt less like a skill and more like a magic trick—abracadabra, and somehow I was wedged between two cars without a scratch. By the end of the course, I felt like I had graduated from a circus school rather than a driver's ed class. I emerged with my learner's permit, ready to hit the road, but I still had a nagging suspicion that my driving skills were best suited for a video game rather than real life.

Looking back, that driver education class taught me not just how to drive, but how to embrace the chaos of life. Because if you can survive high school driver's ed, you can survive just about anything, including the potholes of adulthood.

https://app.videogen.io/view/dpgbkw

Football Tryouts Today, Urgent Care Visit Tomorrow

So, there I was, standing in front of the high school gym, heart racing like I was about to jump out of an airplane. I mean, who knew trying out for the football team would feel more intimidating than my first date? I could practically hear my own heartbeat echoing in my ears, drowning out the sounds of the other kids laughing and joking around. They looked like they were born for this, while I was just... well, I was just born.

I walked up to the field, and it was like stepping into another universe. The sun was shining, the grass was vibrant, and here I was, a walking disaster in a pair of hand-me-down cleats that were two sizes too big. I could almost hear the shoes mocking me, "You're not ready for this!" They were right. The last time I ran this much was when I was trying to escape a swarm of bees in gym class.

As I stood there, I watched the other guys throw the football around like it was a piece of cake. They were spinning it, catching it, and doing these ridiculous tricks that made it look like they were auditioning for a movie about high school sports. Meanwhile, I was just trying to remember which way to run. I mean, I've seen football on TV, but there's a world of difference between watching Tom Brady throw a touchdown and trying to catch a pass from Timmy "the Human Cannonball," who clearly had some pent-up energy to unleash.

Then came the moment of truth: the coach blew the whistle, and we all gathered around. He started talking about teamwork, dedication, and the importance of giving it your all. I nodded along, but inside, I was thinking, "Isn't this just a glorified game of tag with a ball?" I mean, I was just trying to avoid getting tackled and humiliated in front of my peers.

The first drill was a simple passing exercise. I stood there, waiting for my turn, and when it finally came, I felt like I was on stage at the Oscars. "And the award for the most awkward football throw goes to..." Spoiler alert: it was me. I threw the ball with all my might, but it sailed over the head of the intended receiver and landed in the bushes like it was trying to hide from the shame. The bushes seemed to laugh at me, and I could almost hear them whispering, "What were you thinking?"

But I wasn't about to give up. I picked up the ball, wiped the sweat from my brow, and tried again. This time, I aimed a little lower. The ball spiraled out of my hands, but instead of going to the receiver, it hit the coach right in the stomach. He doubled over, and for a moment, I thought he might need a medic. I stood there, frozen, contemplating whether I should apologize or just run away and change my name.

Finally, we moved on to the tackling drills. Now, I've seen cartoons where people get tackled and pop back up like nothing happened, but let me tell you, reality is different. I was paired with a guy who looked like he could bench press a car. When it was my turn to get tackled, I felt like a rag doll being thrown around by a toddler. I hit the ground, and for a second, I thought I could hear the earth laughing at my misfortune.

By the end of the day, I was exhausted, bruised, and questioning every life choice that had led me to this moment. But the best part? I realized that trying out was more than just about football. It was about stepping out of my comfort zone, embracing the chaos, and finding humor in my epic fails. Sure, I might not make the team, but I'd have a story to tell—one where I bravely faced my fears, tackled my insecurities, and maybe, just maybe, learned that sometimes, it's okay to be the punchline.

https://app.videogen.io/view/icqlpe

The Politics Of The Prom Song

Ah, the high school prom theme song. A title that carries the weight of a thousand teenage dreams and a million awkward slow dances. It's the soundtrack to what we all hope will be a magical night, but let's be real, it's mostly just a cacophony of hormonal chaos, questionable fashion choices, and the inevitable "Did you hear about Jessica and Tyler?" gossip that will echo through the halls for the rest of the year. And here we are, tasked with voting for the theme song. The stakes couldn't be higher, folks.

Now, you might think that selecting a song to encapsulate the essence of prom is as easy as pie. But let me tell you, it's more like trying to bake a soufflé while blindfolded and standing on a rollercoaster. First, there's the initial excitement: "Oh, we're going to vote for the prom theme song? This is going to be epic!" But then you realize that everyone has an opinion, and all those opinions are about as diverse as the toppings on a pizza. You've got your classic romantics who want something timeless. You know, the ones who roll their eyes and say, "Nothing beats 'I Will Always Love You.'" Sure, except for the fact that this is high school, not a Whitney Houston tribute concert.

Then there are the party people, the ones who think prom should be one big rave. "Let's go with 'Uptown Funk'!" they shout, as if the mere mention of that song will magically transform the gymnasium into a dance floor worthy of a Las Vegas nightclub. I mean, I get it. We all want to dance like nobody's watching, but let's not forget that our parents will be chaperoning. The last thing I need is my mom trying to bust a move to Bruno Mars while I'm trying to make eye contact with my crush across the room.

And then, there are the "deep thinkers." You know, the ones who want to pick a song that makes a statement. "What about 'Fight Song'?" they suggest. Because nothing says "Let's celebrate our youth" like a power anthem about overcoming adversity. I can picture it now: a room full of teenagers awkwardly swaying while contemplating their life choices, all to the tune of a song that's supposed to inspire us. "Yes, let's celebrate prom by reflecting on the struggles of life! Who needs fun when you can have a mid-life crisis at seventeen?"

And let's not forget the inevitable write-in votes. You know there's always that one kid who thinks they're clever and suggests a song that is so off-the-wall that you can't help but laugh. "How about 'Baby Shark'?" they say, and suddenly, the room erupts in laughter. But then, a few seconds later, you see the glimmer of realization in their eyes. "Wait, what if it actually wins?" And that's when panic sets in. Because can you imagine? The prom theme song being a catchy children's tune? "Welcome to the prom, where the decor is elegant, the food is questionable, and the music will haunt you for years to come!"

After hours of debate, we finally narrow it down to a few contenders. But before we can cast our votes, someone suggests we create a playlist. "Let's just mix them all together!" Because why not? Let's take the romantic ballads, the party anthems, and the inspirational power songs and throw them into a blender. The result? A musical smoothie that's just as confusing as high school itself.

In the end, the theme song doesn't really matter. It's not about the music; it's about the memories we create, the friendships we strengthen, and the awkward moments we'll laugh about for years to come. So whether we end up dancing to "Uptown Funk" or "Baby Shark," we'll make it our own. Because that's what prom is all about—embracing the chaos and making the best of it, one awkward shuffle at a time.

https://app.videogen.io/view/nhqhjh

Within These Walls: Intramural Sports For All

You know, when I think back to my high school days, one of the most vivid memories that pops into my mind is the sheer chaos of intramural sports. I mean, who doesn't love the idea of a bunch of teenagers, fueled by a mix of overconfidence and complete ignorance, trying to play organized sports? It's like watching a pack of wild animals attempting to follow traffic rules. Spoiler alert: it doesn't go well.

Let's start with the fact that everyone and their grandma decided to join a team. You had the jocks, obviously, who thought this was their shot at reclaiming their glory days, even though they peaked in middle school. Then there were the nerds, who showed up in their glasses and knee-high socks, convinced that their knowledge of the game from video games would translate into actual athletic prowess. And let's not forget the kids who just wanted to get out of class and thought showing up in a mismatched uniform would somehow make them athletes. I swear, one guy wore flip-flops to a soccer match. Flip-flops! It was like watching a flamingo try to play football.

Now, let's talk about the sports themselves. We had everything from dodgeball to ultimate frisbee, which, by the way, is a sport that really should come with a warning label: "May cause injury to your pride and your face." I remember the first time I stepped onto the dodgeball court. The adrenaline was pumping, and I was ready to unleash my inner athlete. But instead of channeling my inner Serena Williams, I just ended up dodging balls like I was in a low-budget action movie. I mean, how do you even get hit in the face by a dodgeball when you're actively trying to avoid it? It's a skill, I tell you.

And the rules! Oh, the glorious, chaotic rules. Nobody knew them, and we all pretended we did. "Is it seven hits and you're out?" "No, it's three, but only if you're wearing blue!" I swear, the only rule we all agreed on was that the last person standing got to claim victory, but even that turned into a brawl over who actually caught the ball. I remember one game where we had a full-on debate about whether a ball that grazed your shoulder counted as a hit. It was like a courtroom drama, but with more sweat and less dignity.

And then there were the uniforms. Oh, the uniforms! You'd think we were preparing for the Olympics with the amount of effort we put into them. One team decided to wear matching tie-dye shirts, which looked more like a failed art project than a team uniform. I still have nightmares about that. And my team? We thought we were clever by wearing all black, like we were some kind of ninja squad. Spoiler: we looked less like ninjas and more like a funeral procession that had lost its way.

Let's not forget the "coaching" aspect. We had this one kid who fancied himself a coach. He would stand on the sidelines, yelling advice that was about as useful as a screen door on a submarine. "Just run faster!" he'd shout, as if we hadn't already figured out that running was a key component of sports. Thanks, Coach Obvious. I'll be sure to keep that in mind while I'm tripping over my own shoelaces.

But despite the utter madness and the questionable athleticism, there was something magical about those games. The laughter, the camaraderie, the shared misery of losing spectacularly—it all brought us together. We were a bunch of misfits, trying to figure out how to play sports and navigate the awkwardness of high school at the same time. And in the end, it didn't really matter who won or lost. What mattered was that we showed up, we tried, and we made memories that would last a lifetime. Even if those memories were mostly of me getting hit in the face with a dodgeball.

https://app.videogen.io/view/sntfze

Church Friends, School Friends: Parallel Universes

You know, there's something uniquely hilarious about having both church friends and high school friends in your life at the same time. It's like living in two parallel universes that occasionally collide, and when they do, it's like watching a rom-com where the lead characters have no idea they're in a comedy.

Let's start with the church friends. Now, don't get me wrong; I love them. They're the kind of people who can turn a simple potluck into a full-blown festival. I mean, have you ever seen someone get that excited over a casserole? It's like they're competing for the "Best Dish" award at the Oscars. And the way they pray? It's like they've been rehearsing for a Broadway show. "Dear Heavenly Father, we come before you today..." and I'm just sitting there thinking, "Wow, do I need to take notes? Is there going to be a quiz later?"

And then there's the whole vibe of church friends. They're the kind of people who can turn a casual conversation about the weather into a deep theological discussion. "Oh, it's a beautiful day! God's creation is truly magnificent!" Meanwhile, I'm over here just trying to figure out if I should wear my sandals or my sneakers. And don't get me started on their enthusiasm for volunteering. "Let's go help the needy!" they say, while I'm just trying to muster the energy to help myself to a second slice of pie at the church picnic.

Now, let's switch gears to high school friends. These are the people who understand the true meaning of chaos. They're the ones who can turn a Friday night into an adventure that probably should have come with a warning label. You've got the friend who always suggests the wildest ideas, like going to that sketchy diner at 2 AM because "it's an experience." And you're sitting there, half asleep, wondering how you ended up in a car filled with fast-food wrappers and questionable life choices.

But the best part is when these two worlds collide. Picture this: you're at a church event, and suddenly, your high school friend shows up. They're wearing a band t-shirt that's definitely not church-appropriate, and you can feel the tension in the air. Your church friends are giving you side-eye like you just brought a pet snake to a baptism. "Is that... is that a Metallica shirt?" one of them whispers, clutching their Bible like it's a shield. Meanwhile, your high school friend is trying to engage in a conversation about the latest TikTok trends, completely oblivious to the fact that they've just walked into a scene straight out of a sitcom.

And let's not forget the conversations that ensue when you try to explain your dual life. "So, you go to church every Sunday?" your high school friend asks, eyebrows raised. "Aren't you, like, supposed to be out partying or something?" And I'm just standing there, trying to navigate this minefield of expectations. "Well, yes, but I also bake cookies for the bake sale, and we have a really great choir." It's like trying to explain the plot of a movie that's a mix of horror, romance, and comedy all at once.

Then there are the inevitable questions. "So, do your church friends know about your high school friends?" It's like they're asking if I'm leading a double life, like I'm some kind of superhero with a secret identity. "Well, sort of. But if they found out about the karaoke nights and the late-night fast-food runs, I might have to resign from my position as the church's unofficial cupcake ambassador."

In the end, having church friends and high school friends is like juggling flaming torches while riding a unicycle. It's chaotic, it's messy, and sometimes you just want to throw your hands up and laugh.

Because really, who knew that navigating friendships could feel like a spiritual journey and a wild rollercoaster ride all at once?

https://app.videogen.io/view/nowdeu

Cafeteria-Grade Adventures

You ever walk into a high school cafeteria and think, "Wow, this is the pinnacle of fine dining?" Yeah, me neither. I mean, the moment you step in, it's like entering a culinary battlefield. You've got the smell of mystery meat wafting through the air, mingling with whatever they're calling pizza that day. Seriously, I once saw a slice of pizza that looked like it had been through an existential crisis. It was a sad little triangle, barely holding itself together. I half expected it to start reciting poetry about lost toppings.

And then there's the lunch lady. Now, I don't know if she's a trained professional or a secret agent sent to keep us from eating anything remotely nutritious, but she's out there, slinging mashed potatoes that look like they were made from the last surviving potato on Earth. I swear, I've seen her wield a ladle like a sword, ready to defend her territory against anyone who dares ask for extra gravy. "Extra gravy? You think this is a five-star restaurant? You get one scoop, and that's it!"

You ever notice how the food has a personality? Like, the green beans are always that weird kid in the back of the class, just sitting there, ignored. Nobody wants to touch them. It's like they're the social outcasts of the cafeteria. Meanwhile, the chicken nuggets are the popular kids, strutting around in their crispy coats, getting all the love. "Oh, look at me! I'm shaped like a dinosaur! I'm so cool!" And there's that one kid who's always trying to get the attention of the nuggets, but they just won't give him the time of day. He's stuck with the green beans, and you can see the heartbreak in his eyes.

And the trays! Why are those trays designed like they were made for a Tetris tournament? You've got your mashed potatoes in one compartment, your jiggly fruit cup in another, and then there's that slice of pizza trying to escape its fate. It's like a game of Jenga, except if you mess up, you don't just lose; you end up with a lap full of spaghetti. And don't even get me started on the milk. Is it just me, or does it taste like it was harvested from a cow that only drank soda? I mean, who thought, "Let's serve chocolate milk that's more chocolate than milk?" It's like drinking a candy bar, and you can feel your teeth screaming for mercy.

Then there's the social hierarchy of the cafeteria. You've got the jocks at one table, the drama club at another, and the nerds huddled in the corner, probably discussing the latest superhero movie. And here I am, just trying to find a place to sit, dodging flying food like I'm in some sort of cafeteria dodgeball tournament. "Watch out! Incoming meatball!" It's a whole new level of survival skills. You've got to be quick on your feet, or you'll end up with spaghetti in your hair.

And the conversations! You ever overhear a group of kids discussing their weekend plans while munching on a questionable taco? "I'm going to the mall!" "I'm going to a party!" Meanwhile, I'm just sitting there, contemplating the meaning of life as I stare at a rubbery piece of chicken that's somehow both overcooked and undercooked at the same time. It's a culinary paradox!

But you know what? Despite the chaos, the questionable food choices, and the social minefield, there's something oddly comforting about it all. It's a rite of passage, a shared experience. We're all in this together, navigating the ups and downs of cafeteria cuisine. So here's to the high school cafeteria—where the food might be questionable, but the memories are priceless.

https://app.videogen.io/view/oaiskj

Let The Pidgins Loose: Foreign Language Classes

I remember stepping into my first foreign language class in high school, a place where dreams of becoming a polyglot danced in my head, only to be swiftly crushed by the reality of conjugating verbs. I had signed up for Spanish, thinking it would be a breeze, you know, "Hola! Como estas?" I was practically fluent! Little did I know that my high school Spanish experience would turn into a comedy of errors that would make even the most seasoned stand-up comedian cringe.

The first day of class, I was filled with confidence. I had watched enough telenovelas to believe I could charm my way through any conversation. But as soon as the teacher walked in, I realized I was in over my head. She started speaking at lightning speed, and all I could do was nod and smile, hoping she didn't ask me anything. I felt like I had just entered the Spanish version of "The Hunger Games"—may the odds be ever in your favor, and may you never have to speak a word.

Then came the vocabulary quizzes. Oh, the vocabulary quizzes! They were like mini pop quizzes on my sanity. I still remember the time I was supposed to translate "I like to eat apples" into Spanish. Simple enough, right? But when I stood up to answer, all I could think was, "Manzana... no, that's not right... wait, is it 'me gusta' or 'me gusta mucho'?!" In my panic, I blurted out, "Me gusta la manzana!" The class erupted in laughter, and I realized I had just declared my love for the apple rather than my preference for eating it. Who knew apples could be so romantic?

And let's not forget about the infamous group presentations. You know, the ones where you're supposed to work with your classmates to create a skit in Spanish? My partner and I decided to do a scene at a restaurant. I thought I was nailing it, confidently ordering "dos tacos" and "una cerveza," only to realize halfway through that I was supposed to be the waiter. So there I was, dressed as a waiter in my mind, while my partner was enthusiastically pretending to eat tacos that didn't exist. The only thing I served that day was a hearty helping of embarrassment, garnished with a side of confusion.

The highlight of my language journey, however, had to be the annual language fair. Each year, students were encouraged to showcase their skills, and I thought, "Why not go big?" I decided to perform a song in Spanish. I picked a classic, "La Bamba." I practiced for weeks, convinced I was going to be the next international sensation. The day of the fair arrived, and as I took the stage, I felt a surge of adrenaline. I opened my mouth to sing, and instead of "Para bailar la Bamba," I belted out "Para bailar la banana!" The audience was in stitches, and I was left wondering if I should start a new career as a fruit-themed musician.

But maybe the most memorable part of taking foreign language classes was the friendships forged through our collective struggle. We were all in the same boat, paddling upstream against the current of grammar rules and pronunciation pitfalls. I'll never forget the time we banded together to study for a final exam. We formed a study group, armed with flashcards and snacks, only to spend more time laughing at our mispronunciations than actually studying. "¿Dónde está la biblioteca?" became our inside joke, a phrase that would haunt us long after the class ended.

In the end, while I may not have emerged as the fluent Spanish speaker I envisioned, I did leave high school with a treasure trove of hilarious memories and a newfound appreciation for the complexities of language. So here's to foreign language classes—the awkward moments, the unexpected laughter, and the realization that sometimes, the best way to learn is to embrace the chaos and just roll with the punches. Or, in my case, roll with the manzanas.

https://app.videogen.io/view/deqbpr

Driving Mr. Lazy: The Student Parking Lot

It was the dawn of a new era, the day I finally got to drive myself to high school. I had imagined this moment for years, fantasizing about the freedom, the independence, the sheer thrill of not having to wait for my parents to drop me off. The day arrived, and I was ready. I could already feel the wind in my hair, the sun shining down, and the adoration of my peers as I rolled up in my trusty, old sedan. I mean, who wouldn't want to be seen in a car that looked like it had seen more high school drama than I had?

I remember the moment I got the keys. My dad handed them over like they were the keys to a kingdom. "You're responsible now," he said, and I nodded, trying to suppress the urge to laugh. Responsible? Me? I could barely keep track of my homework, let alone a vehicle. But there was no turning back. I hopped into the driver's seat, adjusted the mirrors, and took a deep breath. It was time to conquer the asphalt jungle.

I backed out of the driveway, feeling like a hero in an action movie. The world was my oyster, or at least my small suburban neighborhood was. I turned on the radio, blasting my favorite tunes, and for a moment, I was invincible. That is until I realized I had no idea how to navigate the labyrinth of streets that led to my school. My GPS, bless its heart, had the patience of a saint as I made three wrong turns and ended up in a coffee shop parking lot. I could practically hear it sighing, "Recalculating…"

After what felt like an eternity of detours, I finally found the road to my high school. I pulled up to the entrance, feeling like I was on the red carpet. My heart raced as I spotted my friends. "Look at me!" I wanted to shout, but instead, I just waved awkwardly, trying to play it cool while simultaneously praying I wouldn't misjudge the distance and hit the curb.

I parked, or at least I thought I parked. I stepped out of the car, and for a moment, I felt like a celebrity stepping out of a luxury vehicle, but then I looked back at my car. It was parked at an angle that would make a geometry teacher weep. I mean, who knew parallel parking could be so complicated? I could practically hear the whispers of my classmates, "Is that a new car? Why is it parked like that?" Spoiler alert: it wasn't new, and it was parked like a toddler had taken the wheel.

As I walked into school, I felt a mix of pride and embarrassment. I was a driver now, but I was also the kid with the car that looked like it had survived a demolition derby. I could hear the chatter: "Did you see her car? It's so... unique!" Unique? That's one way to put it. I chuckled to myself, thinking maybe I'd start a trend. "Vintage chic" could be my new aesthetic.

The day went on, filled with the usual high school chaos: classes, lunch, and the occasional awkward run-in with my crush, who, by the way, had no idea I existed until I rolled up in my automotive masterpiece. I could see him glancing at me, probably wondering if I was a car enthusiast or just someone who had lost a bet.

When the final bell rang, I sprinted to my car, eager to escape the madness of high school. I hopped in, turned on the engine, and felt that familiar rush of freedom. Sure, my car might not have been the coolest ride on the block, but it was mine. And as I drove home, I realized that driving myself to school wasn't just about the car; it was about the journey, the laughter, and the little moments that made high school memorable. Even if my car was a rolling punchline, it was still my punchline, and I wouldn't trade it for anything.

https://app.videogen.io/view/mtbtyp

Letter From An After-School Detention Room

Detention, that infamous rite of passage, a sentence handed down by the high school judicial system for crimes ranging from the egregious act of being late to class to the heinous offense of chewing gum in the wrong place. I remember the day I found myself in the hallowed halls of detention, a place where time stretches like a rubber band, and the air is thick with the scent of regret and stale pizza. I walked in, a fresh face in a sea of hardened criminals—well, at least that's how they looked. There was the kid in the corner who had clearly mastered the art of looking both bored and threatening, the one who seemed to be auditioning for a role in a low-budget prison movie. Then there was the girl doodling in her notebook, her artistic talents clearly wasted on the likes of us. And let's not forget the kid who had somehow managed to turn his detention time into a personal spa day, complete with headphones and a hoodie that could have doubled as a sleeping bag.

The clock on the wall ticked with a mocking rhythm, each second a reminder of my life choices. I had been sentenced to an hour of silence, and let me tell you, silence in a room full of teenagers is like a ticking time bomb. It's only a matter of time before someone cracks. I was convinced that if I stared at the clock long enough, it would magically turn back time, and I could escape this purgatory. But alas, time is a cruel mistress, and she had other plans.

As I sat there, I began to reflect on how I ended up in this predicament. Was it my fault that I had a penchant for witty comebacks? Apparently, telling my history teacher that his lectures were as exciting as watching paint dry wasn't the best way to win favor. Who knew? I thought I was just contributing to the classroom discourse. But here I was, a prisoner of my own sarcasm, surrounded by my fellow inmates, each with their own tales of woe.

The girl doodling in her notebook suddenly burst out laughing, and for a brief moment, I thought, "Yes! The silence has been broken!" But no, she was just showing the kid next to her her latest masterpiece—a stick figure with an exaggerated frown, clearly depicting our detention experience. I couldn't help but chuckle. It was a small act of rebellion, and in that moment, I felt a little less alone.

Then there was the kid who had been silent the entire hour. He finally spoke up, his voice barely above a whisper, "This is worse than jail." I nodded in agreement, thinking of all the things I would rather be doing. I could be at home, binge-watching my favorite show, or even doing homework—yeah, that's how bad it was. Detention had a way of making even the most mundane tasks seem like a vacation.

As time dragged on, I started to notice the little things. The way the fluorescent lights flickered like they were trying to communicate an escape plan. The way the ventilation system hummed a tune that sounded suspiciously like the theme from a horror movie. And the smell—oh, the smell! It was a mix of old gym socks and regret, a scent that would haunt me long after I escaped this place.

Finally, the clock struck the hour, and the door swung open. A wave of relief washed over me as I realized I had survived. I emerged from detention like a prisoner released from a maximum-security prison, ready to embrace freedom. I had made it through, armed with stories and a newfound appreciation for the outside world. Maybe, just maybe, detention wasn't all bad. It was a chance to bond with fellow misfits, a place where laughter could break through the monotony. And as I walked out, I couldn't help but think that the next time I was faced with a choice between detention and a witty comeback, I might just choose the comeback—at least until I had to face the consequences again.

https://app.videogen.io/view/vkxdew

Flipping Burgers, Taking Orders, Wearing Polyester

You ever work at a fast food restaurant in high school? If you haven't, let me paint you a picture. It's like being thrust into a high-speed blender of grease, teenage angst, and the occasional existential crisis—all while wearing a polyester uniform that's two sizes too small. I remember the first day I walked in, the smell of fried everything hitting me like a wall. You know that smell, right? It's a mix of regret and sodium. I was greeted by my manager, a guy named Steve, who looked like he hadn't seen daylight since the '90s. He had this wild hair and a mustache that could only be described as 'caterpillar chic.'

"Welcome to the team!" he said, and I thought, "What team? This is not the Olympics." My first task was to learn the menu, which felt like trying to memorize the entire works of Shakespeare—if Shakespeare had written about burgers and fries instead of tragic love stories. I mean, how many ways can you say "double cheeseburger"? But there I was, standing at the counter, trying to look enthusiastic while internally panicking over whether I'd remember how to ring up a combo meal.

And let me tell you, the customers were a whole different level of chaos. You'd think people would be nice when they're hungry, but no, they're hangry. I had a woman come in once, storming up to the counter like she was about to declare war. "I ordered a large fry, not a medium!" she yelled, as if I personally had conspired against her potato desires. I tried to explain that the fries were the same size as my hopes and dreams—both of which were equally deflated—but she wasn't having it. I just nodded and handed her the fries, trying to suppress a laugh because the way she was glaring at me, you'd think I was the one who invented the medium fry.

Then there were the coworkers. Oh boy, the coworkers. We were a motley crew of misfits. There was Jenna, who was convinced she could make a TikTok career out of flipping burgers, and then there was Kevin, who spent his shifts trying to convince us that he could eat a whole 20-piece nugget by himself. Spoiler alert: he could, and he did. It was like watching a train wreck in slow motion. You knew it was bad for him, but you couldn't look away.

And the drive-thru! The drive-thru was its own universe. It was like a game show where the prize was a cold soda and a side of fries. "Welcome to Fast Food Kingdom, where your order is our command!" I'd say, trying to sound cheerful. But as soon as they'd start ordering, it was like they were speaking a different language. "I'll have a number three, but can you make it a combo, but hold the onions, add extra pickles, and make sure the fries are fresh, and oh, can you throw in a sweet tea?" I'd be standing there, nodding along, thinking, "Sure, let me just consult my crystal ball to see if I can fulfill your every whim."

The highlight of my day was always the end of the shift. I'd walk out, uniform drenched in grease, hair smelling like a fryer, and I'd think, "What did I just do for the last five hours?" It was like a bizarre rite of passage. Sure, I was flipping burgers and dealing with cranky customers, but I was also learning life skills—like how to smile through the pain and how to dodge ketchup packets thrown by my friends during our breaks.

So, if you're ever in a fast food joint and see a teenager behind the counter, remember: they're not just serving food; they're surviving a jungle of fries, hormones, and absurdity. And if you're lucky, they might even hand you your order with a side of laughter.

https://app.videogen.io/view/ghwmvs

The Substitute Teacher Dilemma

You know, there's something almost mythical about substitute teachers. They're like unicorns, appearing out of nowhere, and you're never quite sure if they're real or just a figment of your imagination. One minute, you're sitting in class, minding your own business, pretending to pay attention while actually contemplating whether it's too early for a snack, and the next minute, the door swings open, and in walks a substitute. The energy in the room shifts instantly. It's like the moment you realize you're not just in a classroom; you've been thrust into a reality show where the stakes are low, but the comedy is high.

I remember one particularly memorable day when our regular teacher had to take a sudden leave. We all exchanged glances, the kind that says, "Oh boy, here we go." The bell rang, and in walked Mr. Thompson, or at least that's what he claimed his name was. He looked like he had just stumbled out of a time machine from the 1970s, complete with a patterned shirt that could have been a picnic blanket and glasses that were so thick I half-expected him to be able to see into the future. You could tell he was nervous, but we were all too excited to care.

Mr. Thompson shuffled through his papers, fumbling like he was trying to decipher an ancient scroll. He cleared his throat, and we all leaned in, ready for whatever chaos was about to ensue. "Uh, so, I'm your substitute today!" he said, his voice cracking like a teenager going through puberty. "Let's have some fun!" Fun? With a substitute teacher? This was unprecedented. We were all thinking the same thing:

"What kind of fun? The kind that gets us out of doing work, or the kind that gets us sent to the principal's office?"

He started the class by asking us to introduce ourselves, which was a bold move. We were high school students, not a support group. "Hi, I'm Sarah, and I'm just here to survive." "I'm Jake, and I'm pretty sure I'll be a millionaire by 25." The introductions went on, and I could see Mr. Thompson's enthusiasm waning as he realized we were not the energetic bunch he had hoped for. "Okay, okay, let's get started on today's lesson!"

He turned to the whiteboard and promptly wrote down a math equation that looked like it had come from an alien textbook. "So, who can tell me what this means?" Silence. The kind of silence that fills the air when everyone is suddenly very interested in their shoes. Finally, someone piped up, "Uh, can we just play a game instead?"

To our surprise, Mr. Thompson actually considered it. "Well, I suppose we could play a math game. How about 'Math Jeopardy'?" The collective groan that filled the room was epic. "No, Mr. Thompson, we meant, like, a real game." But he was undeterred, and before we knew it, he had transformed our classroom into a bizarre version of a game show.

He split us into teams, and the questions were ridiculous. "What is the square root of... a pizza?" "How many slices are in a full moon?" The questions made no sense, and yet we were laughing so hard that I thought we might actually pass out. By the end of the class, we had learned absolutely nothing, but we had bonded over our shared confusion and amusement.

When the bell finally rang, we all filed out, leaving Mr. Thompson still trying to figure out how to grade our imaginary math game. As we walked away, I couldn't help but think that maybe, just maybe, substitute teachers are the unsung heroes of high school. They come in, shake things up, and remind us that learning doesn't always have to be serious. Sometimes, it can be a chaotic, hilarious adventure that leaves you with stories to tell for years to come.

https://app.videogen.io/view/uuyrbb

Yes, No, Maybe, Yeah Right: Finding a Prom Date

Finding a date for high school prom is like trying to locate a unicorn in a haystack—if the haystack were filled with awkward teenagers and the unicorn was, well, a socially acceptable way to ask someone to go with you. I mean, let's be real here: prom is the pinnacle of high school experiences, the grand finale of teenage awkwardness, and the last chance to make a memorable mistake before you graduate and enter the real world, where you can make even bigger mistakes, like forgetting to pay your taxes.

So, there I was, sitting in the cafeteria, surrounded by my friends who were all too busy planning their promposals like they were orchestrating a Broadway musical. "I'm going to spell out 'Prom?' in giant letters made of cupcakes!" one of them exclaimed, while another was busy printing out a life-sized cutout of their crush's face to hold up at the football game. Meanwhile, I was over here, contemplating whether it was more socially acceptable to ask someone out via text or to just slip a note into their locker like it was 1995.

Now, let's talk about the pressure of finding a date. It's not just about who you want to go with; it's about who will actually say yes. I mean, I could have asked my crush, Sarah, who I've been secretly admiring from afar, but what if she said no? My heart would shatter into a million pieces and I'd have to spend the rest of the year avoiding her in the hallways like she was a math test I hadn't studied for. So, I decided to take a different approach. I made a list of potential candidates, which felt a lot like drafting a fantasy football team.

First up was Mark, the star of the basketball team. He was tall, athletic, and had a smile that could light up a room. But then I remembered that he was also known for his ability to trip over air and miss free throws. So, I crossed him off the list. Next was Lisa, the girl from my math class who had a knack for solving equations faster than I could find my pencil. But every time I tried to talk to her, I ended up sounding like a babbling idiot. Crossed off. Then there was Dave, my best friend, who had the personality of a wet sock. While he was great for moral support, I didn't think showing up to prom with him would exactly scream "cool."

As the days passed, I felt the pressure mounting. My friends were all getting dates, and I was still sitting here like a sad puppy in a pet store window, just waiting for someone to take me home. I tried to channel my inner Casanova, but the only thing I could muster was a half-hearted "Hey, want to go to prom?" that came out more like a question about whether she wanted ketchup on her fries.

Finally, desperation set in. I decided to take a leap of faith and just ask Sarah directly. I practiced in front of the mirror, rehearsing my lines like I was auditioning for a role in a Shakespearean play. "To prom or not to prom, that is the question," I'd say dramatically, only to realize that I sounded more like a dork than a romantic hero.

So, the day came. I walked up to her, heart racing, palms sweaty, and just blurted it out: "Sarah, will you go to prom with me?" I braced myself for the rejection, but instead, she smiled and said yes! I nearly fainted right there.

In that moment, I realized that finding a date for prom wasn't just about the elaborate plans or the perfect proposal. It was about having the courage to ask, even when it felt like jumping off a cliff without a parachute. So, here's to prom, the awkwardness, the laughter, and the unforgettable memories—because even if it's a disaster, at least it'll make for a great story to tell at the reunion.

https://app.videogen.io/view/xjjzzu

Skipping The School Fantastic

It was a Tuesday morning, and I woke up with the kind of enthusiasm usually reserved for a dentist appointment. The sun was shining, birds were chirping, and my bed was calling me like a siren luring sailors to their doom. I lay there, contemplating the existential crisis that is high school. Why do we subject ourselves to this daily grind of monotony? I mean, who needs math when you can calculate how many hours of sleep you can get if you just skip today? Spoiler alert: it's a lot.

So, I made the executive decision to skip class. It felt like I was making a bold political statement. "I am taking a stand against the oppressive regime of Algebra II!" I thought, as I rolled over and buried my head in my pillow. I had it all planned out. I would tell my friends I was "sick." The kind of sick that involves Netflix, snacks, and a blanket fort.

I donned my best "I'm definitely not skipping school" outfit, which consisted of pajamas that I somehow convinced myself looked like a chic ensemble. I could practically hear my mom's voice in my head, "You're going to regret this!" But honestly, what's regret when you have a whole day of freedom ahead of you?

I settled into my blanket fort, armed with popcorn and a remote. The first episode of my favorite show played, and I felt like I had won the lottery. As the plot thickened, I realized my first mistake: I hadn't factored in the guilt. Ah yes, the guilt. It creeps in like an unwanted relative at a family reunion. "What if my teacher notices I'm gone?" "What if my friends think I'm a loser for skipping?" "What if I miss the day they teach how to find X?" Okay, maybe that last one was a stretch, but you get the idea.

Two hours in, I was feeling pretty good about my decision. I was a renegade, a rebel without a cause, a high school dropout (for a day). But then, my phone buzzed. It was my friend Sarah, the class overachiever, who was clearly not skipping. "Hey! We had a pop quiz today! You missed it!" My heart sank. A pop quiz? The one thing I had been dreading? I could almost hear the collective gasps of my classmates as they filled in their answer sheets. I imagined them whispering, "Where's Jason? He must be failing at life. Poor guy."

Panic set in. I had to do damage control. I texted Sarah back, "What did I miss?" She responded with a barrage of information that felt like a foreign language. "The quadratic formula, the Pythagorean theorem, and a surprise lecture on the importance of being present." The importance of being present? Oh, the irony! Here I was, present in my blanket fort, but absent from the classroom where knowledge was supposedly being imparted.

I decided to throw myself into damage control mode. I would need to study like a caffeinated squirrel before the next class. I grabbed my notes and tried to make sense of the chaos that was Algebra II. But instead of focusing on the math, I found myself thinking about how I had traded a day of equations for a day of escapism.

As the hours passed, I learned something profound: skipping class is like eating a whole pizza by yourself. Initially, it feels incredible, but then you realize you're going to have to face the consequences later. I spent the rest of the day in a frenzy, cramming information into my brain like a squirrel preparing for winter.

So, there I was, a high school student who had skipped class, only to realize that sometimes the real lesson is about balance. Yes, sometimes we need to escape, but we also need to show up. I may have missed the quadratic formula, but I learned that every choice has its price. And sometimes, that price is a pop quiz you didn't study for.

https://app.videogen.io/view/nleuyj

Guidance Counselor: That's A Real Job, Right?

I remember the day I walked into the guidance counselor's office, a place that loomed large in the mythology of my high school experience. It was a rite of passage, a necessary pit stop in the chaotic race to adulthood. I had no clue what to expect, but I was armed with a vague sense of dread and a few half-baked ideas about my future. I mean, who doesn't love a good existential crisis served with a side of awkward small talk?

As I stepped through the door, the first thing that hit me was the smell. Imagine a mix of stale coffee, old paper, and the faint scent of desperation. I half expected to see a sign that read, "Welcome to the Land of Unfulfilled Dreams." The walls were plastered with motivational posters that felt like they were mocking me. "Believe in Yourself!" one proclaimed, while another suggested, "Your Future is Bright!" I couldn't help but think, "Yeah, if by bright you mean a dimly lit room filled with uncertainty."

The counselor, Mrs. Thompson, sat behind her desk, which was cluttered with an impressive array of papers, sticky notes, and what looked like the remains of a lunch that had gone rogue. She had the kind of smile that could only be achieved through years of practice, a sort of "I'm here to help you, whether you like it or not" grin. I took a seat, and as I did, I felt like I was being summoned to the principal's office for a crime I hadn't committed yet.

"So, what do you want to do after high school?" she asked, her voice dripping with enthusiasm. I swear I could see the sparkles in her eyes, like she was genuinely excited to be my life coach. I opened my mouth, ready to unleash the glorious, well-thought-out plan I had concocted over the years. But all that came out was, "Um, I don't know. Maybe… something?"

She nodded, as if I had just revealed the meaning of life. "Something! That's a great start!" I could see her scribbling down notes, probably writing "Incredibly Ambitious Student" or "Future President of the World." I wanted to clarify that my "something" was more like "anything that doesn't involve math," but I didn't have the heart to burst her bubble.

Then came the personality tests. Oh, the personality tests! They were like a series of riddles designed to uncover the deepest, darkest secrets of my soul. "If you were an animal, what would you be?" Mrs. Thompson asked, her eyes gleaming with anticipation. I panicked. "Um, a sloth?" I replied, thinking about how I could really get behind the whole "hanging out in trees all day" lifestyle. She jotted something down, probably noting my "laid-back approach to life."

After what felt like an eternity of questions, she leaned back in her chair, looking as if she had just cracked the code to the universe. "You know, I think you'd really thrive in a creative field." Creative field? My mind raced. Was that code for "you're not cut out for anything else"? I couldn't help but picture myself as an artist, living in a tiny studio, surrounded by canvases and the smell of paint, while my bank account dwindled to nothing. "What do you think about graphic design?" she continued, her enthusiasm unwavering. I nodded, trying to look like I was considering a life-changing decision rather than just trying to avoid a future in accounting.

As the meeting wrapped up, she handed me a pamphlet that looked like it had been printed in the '80s. "Here's some information on local colleges!" she chirped. I took it, feeling like I was holding a treasure map to a land I had no desire to explore. I left her office that day with more questions than answers, but at least I had a newfound appreciation for sloths. Who knew that meeting with a guidance counselor could be so enlightening?

https://app.videogen.io/view/civcmv

Nerds, Jocks, Preps, Burn-Outs: That Cliquing Noise

High school is like a giant petri dish of social experiments, where every clique is a distinct strain of bacteria, each with its own quirks, habits, and, let's be honest, a little bit of weirdness. You've got your jocks, who are basically just walking protein shakes, flexing their muscles and their social status like it's an Olympic sport. They strut around the hallways like they own the place, probably because they do—at least until the next pep rally. Their conversations revolve around game stats and how much they can bench press, which is impressive until you realize they can't bench press a book. They're the kings of the cafeteria, ruling over their domain with the power of a thousand chicken nuggets. And let's not forget the cheerleaders, who are basically the jocks' cheer squad and also the queens of the social hierarchy. They have perfected the art of the high-pitched giggle and the dramatic hair flip, which, let's be honest, is probably a form of cardio in itself.

Then there are the nerds, who are the unsung heroes of high school. You can find them huddled together in the library, discussing the latest Marvel movie or the intricacies of quantum physics. They're the ones who will eventually rule the world, but right now, they're just trying to survive the cafeteria's meatloaf day. Their idea of a wild Friday night is a Dungeons & Dragons marathon, and honestly, they're living their best lives. They've got their own lingo, which sounds like a mix between a foreign language and a secret code. You might catch a glimpse of them in the hall, wearing matching graphic tees and thick-rimmed glasses, and you can't help but admire their dedication to their craft.

And speaking of dedication, let's talk about the goths. They're like the dark, brooding poets of the high school ecosystem, draped in black and armed with eyeliner that could probably double as a weapon. They walk around with a sense of melancholy that's both intriguing and slightly intimidating. You can always spot them by their love for all things macabre and their uncanny ability to quote Edgar Allan Poe at the drop of a hat. They're the ones who will sit in the corner of the cafeteria, sipping their black coffee and contemplating the meaning of life while the rest of us are just trying to figure out where to sit without looking like total losers.

Then we have the hipsters, who are basically the trendsetters of the school—if only they could agree on what's actually trendy. They're always a step ahead, sporting thrift store finds and artisanal snacks that no one else has ever heard of. They'll sip their cold brew coffee while discussing the merits of vinyl records over digital music, and you can't help but think they're living in a different decade. They're the ones who will tell you that your favorite band is "too mainstream," while they're blasting some obscure indie artist that no one else can pronounce.

And let's not forget about the popular kids, who seem to float above the rest of us like a group of social angels. They're the ones with the perfect hair, the perfect clothes, and the perfect Instagram feeds. They're always in the spotlight, and somehow, they manage to make it look effortless. You can spot them in the cafeteria, laughing a little too loudly at their inside jokes, while the rest of us sit back and wonder how they got so many followers.

In the end, high school is a melting pot of personalities, and each clique brings its own flavor to the table. Whether you're a jock, a nerd, a goth, a hipster, or a popular kid, we all have one thing in common: we're just trying to navigate the chaos and figure out who we are in this wild social experiment. So, here's to the cliques, the misfits, and everyone in between—because high school wouldn't be half as entertaining without all the glorious weirdness we bring to the table.

https://app.videogen.io/view/xzmmhb

Letting Your Freak Flag Fly

You know, being different in high school is like being a unicorn in a field full of horses. You prance in all sparkly and colorful, and everyone else is just munching on grass, oblivious to the magic you bring. But trust me, that sparkly coat? It attracts attention, and not always the good kind.

I remember my first day of high school, stepping through those double doors, heart pounding like I was about to take the stage at the Oscars. I had my vintage band T-shirt on, the one that was two sizes too big, and a pair of combat boots that had seen more action than a soldier in the trenches. I thought I looked cool. I thought I looked different. Turns out, I looked like I just crawled out from under a rock, and not the cool kind of rock—more like the one that's been sitting in the back of someone's garage for years.

The first few weeks were a whirlwind of awkward encounters and puzzled looks. I'd walk into the cafeteria, and it felt like the entire room would pause, forks hovering in mid-air, as if I had just announced I was the new principal. I'd sit down at a table, and it was like I had thrown a grenade into a peaceful picnic. Suddenly, everyone was whispering and giggling behind their hands. I could almost hear the thoughts bouncing around: "Who does she think she is?" "Why is she dressed like that?" "Is she going to start a revolution?"

I was, of course, just trying to be myself. But in high school, being yourself is like wearing a neon sign that says, "Look at me! I'm different!" And, let's be honest, being different isn't always a walk in the park; sometimes, it's more like a stumble through a minefield.

Take gym class, for example. I was never the athletic type. My idea of exercise was running to the fridge during commercial breaks. So, when they announced a dodgeball tournament, I thought, "Great! An opportunity to showcase my incredible ability to dodge responsibility!" But no, I was thrust into the game like a sacrificial lamb. I stood there, dodging balls like I was in some sort of twisted action movie, while the jocks were out there throwing them like they were training for the Olympics. I remember one of them, a guy named Chad—of course his name was Chad—threw a ball that hit me square in the face. I didn't just dodge the ball; I dodged dignity, self-respect, and probably a few brain cells.

And let's not even get started on prom. Oh, prom. The pinnacle of high school socializing. I had this grand idea of going in a bright purple dress with a giant tulle skirt, the kind that could double as a parachute. I thought it would be fun, quirky, and a statement of my individuality. But when I walked in, it was like I had arrived at a funeral dressed as a clown. Everyone else was in sleek black or shimmering pastels, and there I was, looking like I'd just come from a fairy tale gone horribly wrong.

But here's the kicker: the more they stared, the more I embraced it. I realized that being different was my superpower. I was the unicorn in a world of horses, and I could either hide my sparkle or let it shine. So, I started to own it. I wore my vintage shirts with pride, danced like nobody was watching (even though they were), and laughed at the absurdity of it all.

By the time graduation rolled around, I had learned that being different wasn't just about standing out; it was about standing tall. I might not have fit into their mold, but I had created my own, and it was a whole lot more fun. So here's to the misfits, the weirdos, and the unicorns out there—keep prancing, keep shining, and for goodness' sake, dodge those dodgeballs!

https://app.videogen.io/view/pxuweg

The Mr. Holland's Opus Club

You know, when I think back to high school, I can't help but chuckle at the parade of teachers who shaped my life in ways I didn't even fully appreciate at the time. It's like a sitcom where each character is more eccentric than the last, and somehow, I was the unwitting audience member, just trying to survive algebra while navigating the social minefield of teenage angst.

Let's start with Mr. Thompson, our history teacher. Now, Mr. Thompson had this uncanny ability to turn even the most mundane historical facts into a dramatic reenactment. I swear, he could make the signing of the Declaration of Independence sound like an episode of "Survivor." He'd pace around the classroom, waving his arms like he was conducting an orchestra, and we'd all sit there, half-amused, half-confused, wondering if we were supposed to take notes or just enjoy the show. "And then, Jefferson said, 'We hold these truths to be self-evident!'" He'd shout, and we'd all nod like we were witnessing the birth of a nation instead of just sitting in a cramped classroom.

Then there was Ms. Jenkins, the English teacher who had a passion for Shakespeare that bordered on obsession. She had this way of making us read the most complicated texts, and by the end of it, I was convinced that Shakespeare was just a fancy way of saying, "Let's make this as confusing as possible." Ms. Jenkins would always ask, "What do you think Hamlet is really feeling?" And I'd sit there, trying to remember if I had even read the play or just watched a bad movie adaptation. But she had this infectious enthusiasm that made me want to participate, even when I had no idea what was going on. "It's all about the existential dread!" she'd exclaim, and I'd think, "Well, that explains my entire high school experience!"

And then there was Coach Miller, the gym teacher. Now, Coach Miller was a legend—not because of his coaching skills, but because he had this uncanny ability to turn any game into a life lesson. "Life is like dodgeball!" he'd yell, as we ducked and dodged for our lives. "Sometimes you get hit, but it's how you get back up that counts!" I mean, come on, Coach. I just got smacked in the face with a rubber ball. I'm not exactly feeling inspired here. But somehow, he made us feel like gladiators, ready to conquer the world, even if we were just trying to avoid getting hit in the head by a flying ball.

And let's not forget about Mrs. Patel, the science teacher who was convinced that we could all become the next great scientists of our generation. She'd come into class with her wild hair and oversized lab coat, ready to conduct experiments that usually ended up with us covered in glitter or baking soda. "Today, we're going to create a volcano!" she'd announce, and we'd all roll our eyes, thinking, "Great, another mess to clean up." But by the end of the class, when the "volcano" erupted in a glorious explosion of vinegar and baking soda, we were all cheering like we'd just discovered a new element. "See? Science is fun!" she'd say, and I'd think, "Sure, until I have to clean it up!"

As I look back, I realize that these teachers weren't just educators; they were characters in the great comedy of my teenage years. They taught me that learning didn't have to be a chore and that life was full of unexpected moments. They made me laugh, cringe, and sometimes even question my sanity, but they also made me appreciate the absurdity of it all. So here's to the teachers who turned history into drama, literature into existential crises, gym class into life lessons, and science into a messy adventure. They may not have known it, but they were the stars of my high school sitcom, and I wouldn't trade those memories for anything.

https://app.videogen.io/view/gjegqp

As The Paint Dries: Study Hall Memories

Ah, study hall, the sacred sanctuary of high school life. It's that magical hour carved out of the chaotic school day where the bell tolls, and suddenly, the halls are filled with the muffled sounds of a thousand students pretending to be productive. You walk in, and it's like entering a parallel universe where time stands still and the only currency is procrastination. The desks are arranged in a haphazard way, as if they were thrown in by a tornado of apathy, and the air is thick with the scent of stale cafeteria food and desperation.

You settle into your seat, and the first thing you notice is that the clock on the wall is not your friend. It ticks away slowly, each second a reminder of how little you want to be here. You glance around the room, and there's always that one kid in the corner who's actually studying. You know, the overachiever with perfect grades and a backpack that looks like it's been packed by a professional organizer. They sit there, surrounded by their color-coded notes and highlighters, while the rest of us are busy crafting elaborate daydreams about what we could be doing instead of this.

Next to you, there's the duo of best friends who have turned study hall into their own personal gossip column. They've got the latest scoop on who's dating whom, and it's like watching a soap opera unfold in real time. "Did you hear about Jessica and Matt? Apparently, they broke up because he didn't share his fries!" The drama is riveting, and suddenly, you're invested in their lives more than your own algebra homework. You might even find yourself nodding along, completely forgetting that you're supposed to be studying for that very algebra test you've been avoiding.

Then there's the kid who somehow manages to fall asleep every single study hall. You know the one. They've perfected the art of the head bob, a delicate dance between consciousness and oblivion. One moment they're upright, and the next, their head is lolling to the side, drooling slightly on their desk. You can't help but admire their dedication to napping. It's a skill, really. You wonder if they're dreaming of a world where study hall doesn't exist—where there are no awkward silences and no need to pretend you're working on that history project that's due tomorrow.

And let's not forget the teacher who supervises this circus. They sit at the front, a watchful guardian of chaos, armed with a stack of worksheets and an unyielding determination to keep the peace. You can see them trying to maintain an air of authority, but it's like herding cats. They make the occasional attempt to shush the room, but it's met with a collective eye roll. "You're supposed to be studying!" they say, but it's like trying to convince a cat to take a bath. The students are resolute in their mission to do anything but study.

You pull out your own homework, staring at the paper as if it's written in an ancient language. You know you should be working, but instead, you find yourself scrolling through your phone, watching videos of cats doing ridiculous things. It's a slippery slope, and before you know it, you've lost half the period to a rabbit hole of internet absurdity. You glance up at the clock, and it's only been five minutes.

Finally, the bell rings, and just like that, the spell is broken. You pack up your things, feeling a mix of relief and disappointment. You've survived another study hall, and while you may not have accomplished anything remotely academic, you've gathered enough gossip to fill a novel and witnessed the art of napping in its purest form. As you shuffle out, you can't help but think that maybe, just maybe, study hall isn't about studying at all. It's a rite of passage, a social experiment, and a reminder that sometimes, the best lessons aren't found in textbooks, but in the chaos of teenage life.

https://app.videogen.io/view/elhtjx

My Locker, My Life

Ah, the high school locker. A metal box that holds the essence of teenage life, a monument to the chaos of adolescence. If you think about it, it's the perfect metaphor for high school itself: cramped, filled with a mishmash of emotions, and somehow always smelling faintly of gym socks and regret. I mean, who came up with the idea of assigning every student a tiny, personal storage unit? It's like giving a raccoon its own apartment—sure, it's cute in theory, but in practice, it's just a disaster waiting to happen.

Let's start with the sheer excitement of getting your locker assigned. You walk in on the first day, and there it is, a shiny number on a piece of paper, like winning the lottery. "Congratulations! You are now the proud owner of Locker 237!" You feel a rush of pride, like you've just been given the keys to a castle. But then you approach it, and reality hits. It's not a castle; it's a rusty, dented hunk of metal that's seen more drama than a daytime soap opera. You try to open it, and it's like the universe is conspiring against you. The lock is jammed, and you're standing there, fumbling with the combination like it's a secret code to the vault of a bank. "Is it left to 30? Or was it right to 10? Oh, forget it, I'll just leave my gym clothes in my backpack forever."

And let's talk about what's inside. If you're anything like me, your locker quickly becomes a black hole of forgotten items. I once found a sandwich in mine that had grown its own ecosystem. I'm pretty sure it was the birthplace of a new species. You know it's bad when your friends start calling it "The Science Project." I had a whole semester's worth of notes crammed in there, but let's be real—who needs notes when you can just wing it and hope for the best? The only thing I ever pulled out of that locker was a crumpled piece of paper that said, "Remember to breathe," and honestly, that's the best advice I ever got in high school.

Then there's the social aspect of the locker. It's like your personal stage where you perform the daily drama of high school. You open it, and suddenly, it's a magnet for all your friends. "What's in there?" they ask, peering inside as if it's the treasure chest of a pirate. "Oh, just my dreams and aspirations," I'd say, while internally I'm thinking, "More like my gym shoes and a half-eaten granola bar." And the conversations that happen at lockers! It's like a soap opera. "Did you hear about Sarah and Jake?" "No way! What happened?" "They broke up because he borrowed her favorite pencil and never gave it back!" The locker becomes a confessional, a gossip hub, and a storage unit all in one. It's where friendships are forged and broken, all while trying to navigate the minefield of who borrowed whose favorite hoodie.

And let's not forget the ultimate tragedy: the locker slam. You know what I'm talking about. You're having a rough day, you're late for class, and in a moment of sheer frustration, you slam that locker door shut like you're auditioning for the role of an angry teenager in a movie. But then, the realization hits you: you've just locked your backpack inside. There you stand, staring at the door as if it's betrayed you. "How could you do this to me, Locker 237? I thought we had something special!"

In the grand scheme of life, high school lockers are just a blip on the radar. But in those four years, they become a part of your identity, a reflection of your journey. So here's to the high school locker: a metal box that held our secrets, our snacks, and our sanity. It may be a chaotic mess, but it's a mess we all survived, and somehow, it made us who we are today.

https://app.videogen.io/view/bqyrhx

Senior Pranks: The Good, The Bad, And The Misdemeanor

Ah, senior pranks, the glorious rite of passage that every high school senior dreams of. You know, the kind of shenanigans that make you feel like a rebellious mastermind, the kind of antics that will be remembered in the hallowed halls of your alma mater for decades to come. I mean, what's more thrilling than the thought of leaving your mark on a place that's been your second home for four years? But let's be honest: most of us don't have the creativity of a Picasso or the planning skills of a heist movie director. Instead, we have a bunch of kids armed with a few rolls of duct tape, some balloons, and a questionable sense of humor.

Take my high school, for instance. Our senior class was a mix of overachievers, slackers, and that one kid who always had a pet goldfish in his backpack. You know the type. So, when it came time to plan the senior prank, we had a brainstorming session that looked more like a therapy group for frustrated comedians. Ideas flew around like confetti at a New Year's party. Someone suggested filling the principal's office with balloons, which, let's be real, is about as original as a cat meme. Another genius proposed swapping the cafeteria's meatloaf with a giant cake shaped like a meatloaf. Why? Because nothing says "I'm a responsible adult" like a meat-flavored dessert.

Eventually, we settled on a classic: the old "toilet paper the school" routine. It's a timeless tradition, right? But as we plotted our course of action, it became painfully clear that we were not the stealthy ninjas we imagined ourselves to be. We were more like a group of clumsy elephants trying to tiptoe through a field of landmines. Our first challenge? The logistics. Who knew that unrolling several hundred feet of toilet paper could be so complicated? It's like trying to solve a Rubik's Cube while riding a unicycle. We had one guy who was supposed to be our lookout, but he got distracted by a squirrel. A SQUIRREL! I mean, come on, we're trying to pull off a heist here, not audition for a nature documentary.

So, there we were, armed with rolls of TP, creeping around the school like we were in a spy movie, except instead of cool gadgets, we had a pocketful of Charmin. And then, of course, there was the inevitable moment of panic when we heard the sound of footsteps. Our lookout, who had finally returned from his squirrel chase, yelled, "Run!" And in that instant, we turned into Olympic sprinters, except we weren't sprinting toward the finish line; we were racing to avoid getting caught by the janitor. I swear, that man had the reflexes of a cat.

We made it back to the parking lot, hearts racing, adrenaline pumping, and feeling like we had just successfully robbed Fort Knox. But then came the moment of truth. The next day, we arrived at school, and as we rounded the corner, our hearts sank. Instead of a glorious display of toilet paper cascading down the trees like a winter wonderland, we were greeted by the sight of a barren landscape. Apparently, the janitor had a PhD in toilet paper removal because everything was spotless. It was like we hadn't even tried.

But that's the beauty of senior pranks, isn't it? They're not really about the execution; they're about the camaraderie, the laughter, and the ridiculous stories you get to tell for years to come. Sure, we may not have succeeded in our mission to cover the school in TP, but we did succeed in creating a memory that would last a lifetime. And honestly, isn't that what high school is all about? So, here's to all the failed pranks, the awkward moments, and the laughter that makes it all worthwhile. Because in the end, it's not about the toilet paper; it's about the friends you make along the way.

https://app.videogen.io/view/oymcvu

High School Art Class: An Alternative Nation-In-Training

Ah, high school art classes, the glorious realm where creativity flourishes, and chaos reigns supreme. I remember walking into that classroom for the first time, surrounded by the scent of paint, the sound of laughter, and the unmistakable aura of impending disaster. It was like stepping into a carnival run by slightly unhinged clowns who all had a degree in "How to Make a Mess." You could practically hear the whispers of tortured souls who had tried to create masterpieces but instead ended up with something resembling a modern art exhibit gone wrong.

Let's talk about the teachers. They were a peculiar breed, weren't they? Our art teacher, Ms. Thompson, had a wild mane of hair that looked like it had been styled by a tornado. She wore oversized glasses that magnified her eyes to the size of saucers, making her look perpetually surprised, as if she had just discovered that paint can stain anything it touches. She would glide around the room, clutching a paintbrush like it was a magic wand, ready to transform our stick figures into something profound. "Art is about self-expression!" she would exclaim, as if self-expression could somehow explain why I had just painted a purple cow with a top hat.

And then there were my classmates. Oh, the characters! There was Jake, the kid who believed he was the next Picasso, but his idea of abstract art involved slapping paint on the canvas and calling it "The Essence of Chaos." He would stand there, arms crossed, nodding sagely as if he were channeling the spirit of the great masters. Meanwhile,

I was just trying to figure out how to draw a straight line without it ending up looking like a drunken snake. Then there was Sarah, the self-proclaimed "artistic genius," who would spend hours painstakingly sketching what she called "the human experience." I'm pretty sure her "human experience" was just a series of sad-looking stick figures with exaggerated frowns. I admired her dedication, though. It takes a special kind of person to turn a simple drawing into an existential crisis.

And let's not forget the supplies. The art room was a treasure trove of chaos. Paints in every color imaginable, all of which had mysteriously turned into a rainbow of goo by the end of the semester. I once found a half-empty bottle of neon green paint that looked like it had been used in a science experiment gone wrong. I had high hopes for it, thinking it would add a pop of color to my project. Instead, it became the highlight of my life as I accidentally knocked it over, creating what could only be described as a toxic swamp on the floor. Ms. Thompson's eyes widened in horror as she watched the green goo spread like a scene from a horror movie. "It's a metaphor for the destruction of nature!" I shouted, desperately trying to redeem myself.

Then there were the critiques. Ah, the critiques! Nothing quite like sitting in a circle, staring at each other's work, trying to come up with something profound to say about a piece that looked like it had been created by a toddler with a sugar high. "Your use of color is... interesting," I would say, while secretly wondering if I could just draw a stick figure and call it a day. And the feedback! "I feel like this piece speaks to the inner turmoil of the soul." Really? Because I was just trying to draw a cat.

But despite the chaos, the mess, and the occasional existential crisis, there was something magical about those art classes. They taught us that creativity doesn't have to be perfect, that it's okay to make a mess, and that sometimes, the best art comes from the most unexpected places. So here's to high school art classes, where chaos and creativity collide, and where every paint-splattered canvas tells a story—usually a very confusing one, but a story nonetheless.

https://app.videogen.io/view/ackfzq

Class Play Theater Of The Absurd

I remember the day I signed up for the high school class play. It was one of those moments where you think, "Why not? How bad could it be?" Spoiler alert: it could be very bad. I was a freshman, wide-eyed and naïve, convinced that I was the next big thing in theater. I had seen my fair share of Broadway shows on YouTube, and I thought, "If they can do it, so can I!" Little did I know, the only thing I was qualified to do was make a fool of myself in front of a crowd.

The play was a classic—some Shakespearean tragedy that I had only skimmed the plot of in the hopes of sounding cultured. I was cast as the lead, which seemed like a great honor until I realized that meant I had to learn actual lines. I had no idea what I was doing. I thought memorizing lines would be like cramming for a math test. Just read it a few times, and voilà! You're a Shakespearean genius. Instead, I found myself standing in front of the mirror, trying to channel my inner Hamlet while simultaneously wondering if I could pull off the brooding look without looking constipated.

Rehearsals were a whirlwind of chaos. Picture a group of teenagers, all trying to take their craft seriously, but also trying to figure out if they'd rather be at the mall or scrolling through TikTok. There was the girl who took it way too seriously, practicing her soliloquies like she was auditioning for the Royal Shakespeare Company, and then there was me, who was just trying to remember the difference between "to be" and "to not be." I swear, I spent more time worrying about my costume than my lines. I mean, how do you convincingly portray a tortured prince when your costume looks like it was borrowed from a 90s garage sale?

The big night arrived with all the pomp and circumstance of a royal wedding—minus the horses and the tiaras, of course. I walked onto that stage, heart racing, palms sweaty, and immediately forgot my first line. I stood there, staring at the audience like a deer caught in headlights, while my mind went completely blank. I could feel the judgment radiating from the front row, where my parents sat, likely questioning their decision to raise me. "Is this what we've come to?" they probably thought. "We paid for acting classes, and this is what we get?"

Finally, I managed to stumble through my lines, but not without a few hiccups. I accidentally called my love interest by the wrong name—let's just say, "Juliet" became "Judy," and the look of confusion on her face was priceless. The audience erupted in laughter. I wanted to crawl into a hole and never come out, but then I realized that the laughter was actually kind of nice. Maybe this was my niche—being the comic relief in a tragic play.

As the performance went on, I started to embrace the chaos. I threw in a few dramatic gestures that were more "over-the-top soap opera" than "Shakespearean tragedy." I could see my drama teacher's face turning red with a mix of horror and disbelief, but hey, at least I was entertaining someone! By the end of the night, I had transformed from a nervous wreck into a full-blown diva, complete with exaggerated accents and wild hand movements.

When the curtain finally fell, I took my bow, and the applause felt like a standing ovation at the Oscars. I may not have nailed the role of a tortured prince, but I had inadvertently created a new genre—tragicomedy, starring yours truly. I walked off that stage, sweaty but triumphant, and I realized that maybe, just maybe, the true art of performance wasn't about perfection. It was about embracing the absurdity, making mistakes, and laughing along the way. And honestly, isn't that what high school is all about?

https://app.videogen.io/view/wkywbz

Oiningjay Atinlay Clubay

You know, when I first heard about the Latin club in high school, I thought it was some sort of secret society where we'd all sit around in togas, sipping grape juice and discussing the finer points of ancient Roman philosophy. I imagined we'd be chanting "Carpe Diem" while plotting world domination or at least figuring out how to get extra credit for our Latin homework. So, naturally, I thought, "Hey, why not? How hard can it be?" Spoiler alert: it was harder than deciphering a cat's mood.

So there I was, bright-eyed and bushy-tailed, walking into the first meeting, fully prepared to embrace my inner Julius Caesar. I had my toga ready, which, let me tell you, was just a bedsheet I'd cleverly draped over my shoulders. I was feeling pretty good about myself until I noticed that no one else was wearing a toga. In fact, they were all dressed like they'd just come from a mathlete competition. I suddenly felt like I'd crashed an AP Calculus study group instead of a gathering of future gladiators.

The club president, who I later learned was a senior with a penchant for quoting Cicero at the most inappropriate times, introduced herself. Her name was Penelope, and she was as enthusiastic about Latin as a cat is about taking a bath. She started talking about the importance of Latin in modern languages, and I nodded along, trying to look wise. But inside, I was thinking, "I can barely handle English; why am I here?"

Penelope handed out sheets of paper with the club's motto: "Veni, Vidi, Vici." I thought it was some sort of ancient Roman battle cry, but it turned out to be the Latin version of "I came, I saw, I conquered." I felt more like "I came, I sat awkwardly, I left." But I was determined to conquer this Latin thing, so I stuck around.

The first activity was a vocabulary quiz. I mean, who doesn't love a good quiz, right? I sat at a table with a bunch of kids who looked like they'd just come from a Shakespearean play rehearsal. They were throwing around terms like "et tu, brute" and "cogito, ergo sum" as if they were discussing the latest TikTok trends. I scribbled down random words like "pasta" and "pizza," because, you know, they're derived from Latin. Spoiler alert: they weren't on the quiz.

After the quiz, we played a game called "Latin Jeopardy." Now, I don't know about you, but when I think of a fun game night, I don't immediately think of conjugating verbs. But there I was, standing in front of the board, trying to remember what "amo, amas, amat" meant while simultaneously wondering if I had left the oven on at home. I buzzed in with confidence, thinking I'd nailed it, only to realize I'd just shouted the word for "love" in a room full of people who had clearly never experienced it.

As the weeks went by, I found myself becoming more and more entrenched in this bizarre world of Latin. I learned that "cactus" was actually a Latin word, which made me feel oddly connected to my houseplant. I started using Latin phrases in everyday conversation, much to the confusion of my friends. "Hey, wanna grab pizza?" "Veni, Vidi, Vici, my friend!" They looked at me like I was speaking Klingon.

In the end, I didn't become the next Cicero or even a decent Latin speaker. But I did learn that sometimes, stepping out of your comfort zone leads to unexpected friendships and a newfound appreciation for a language that, let's be honest, is mostly used for naming pizza toppings. So, if you ever find yourself in a high school Latin club, just remember: it's not about conquering a language; it's about embracing the absurdity of it all. Plus, you might just discover that Latin is a lot like high school itself—confusing, a little dramatic, and ultimately, a lot of fun.

https://app.videogen.io/view/bamlcv

Habla Espanol? Me Neither.

When I first heard about the high school Spanish club, I thought, "Why not? It's a chance to practice my Spanish and maybe even impress some people." I mean, how hard could it be? I had just finished a year of Spanish class, and I had learned all the important phrases: "¿Dónde está la biblioteca?" and "Me gusta el helado." Clearly, I was practically fluent. I envisioned myself as the next Antonio Banderas, charming my classmates with my newfound linguistic prowess. Spoiler alert: I was not.

The first meeting was held in the back of the cafeteria, which was basically a glorified storage room with a few folding chairs and a poster of a taco on the wall. I walked in, brimming with enthusiasm, only to be met with the sight of my fellow students chatting away in rapid-fire Spanish. I stood there, the lone English speaker, feeling like a lost puppy at a dog show. I could barely catch a word, and it was then that I realized my Spanish was more "¿Dónde está la biblioteca?" than "Hola, ¿cómo estás?"

As the meeting progressed, the club president, a girl named Isabella, started discussing upcoming events. She spoke with such passion about the "Noche de Cultura," a cultural night where we would showcase our Spanish talents. I felt a wave of panic wash over me. Talents? What talents? I had no idea what I was doing. I could barely remember how to conjugate "hablar" in the past tense. Meanwhile, everyone else was brainstorming ideas for performances, like flamenco dancing and poetry recitals. I was just trying to remember how to say "Hi, my name is" without sounding like I was having a stroke.

Eventually, I decided to contribute. I raised my hand and said, "I can... uh... make guacamole?" The room went silent. I could practically hear crickets chirping. Isabella smiled politely, but I could tell she was thinking, "Great, we've got a culinary genius here." I could feel the weight of my contribution hanging in the air, like a bad burrito. But hey, I thought, at least I'd get to eat some delicious guacamole.

As the weeks went by, I tried to immerse myself in the club. I practiced my Spanish at home, repeating phrases in front of the mirror like a deranged parrot. But every time I entered the club, I felt like I was stepping into a foreign land where everyone spoke a dialect I had never learned. The other members were so enthusiastic, discussing their favorite telenovelas and reggaeton artists, while I was still trying to figure out how to say "I like tacos." I felt like the awkward kid at a dance party, standing against the wall while everyone else was busting out their best moves.

The Noche de Cultura arrived faster than I could prepare. I found myself in front of the club, nervously clutching a bowl of guacamole, which I had made with the utmost care. I was ready to present my masterpiece. As I stepped up to the mic, I thought, "This is it. My moment to shine." I cleared my throat and said, "Hola, soy... uh... I like guacamole." The room erupted in laughter, and I was mortified. But then I realized, maybe that was the point. I was making people laugh, and that was worth something.

By the end of the night, I had learned more than just Spanish; I had learned that it's okay to be a little ridiculous. I may not have left the club fluent, but I did leave with a newfound appreciation for guacamole, a collection of embarrassing stories, and a group of friends who embraced my awkwardness. And honestly, isn't that what high school is all about?

https://app.videogen.io/view/glsukc

Join The French Club, Lose The Attitude

You know, when I decided to join the high school French club, I thought I was signing up for a delightful journey into the world of baguettes, berets, and the occasional existential crisis. I pictured myself sipping café au lait in a quaint Parisian café, while discussing the profound philosophies of Camus and Sartre. Instead, I found myself in a cramped classroom, surrounded by a group of students who were just as clueless about French as I was, but who were all somehow convinced that they would be fluent by the end of the semester. Spoiler alert: we were not.

The first meeting was a whirlwind of excitement. Our club president, who we all assumed had just returned from a year in France, walked in with a scarf that was definitely too long and a confidence that was definitely too misplaced. "Bonjour, mes amis!" she exclaimed, and we all nodded like bobbleheads, because who wouldn't want to be friends with someone who could say "hello" in a language that was already giving us anxiety?

As she launched into a passionate speech about the beauty of the French language, I couldn't help but notice that half the room was already lost. I mean, I was still trying to figure out how to pronounce "bonjour" without sounding like I was choking on a croissant. But there we were, all nodding enthusiastically, pretending we understood every word while secretly Googling "how to say 'I have no idea what you're talking about' in French."

Then came the part of the meeting where we were supposed to introduce ourselves in French. I panicked. My brain went blank. I could barely remember my own name, let alone how to say it in another language. So, I did what any reasonable person would do: I stood up, cleared my throat, and said, "Je m'appelle... um... I like pizza." Yes, that was my big contribution to the French club. I was a culinary genius, apparently.

The club meetings quickly devolved into a series of mispronunciations and awkward attempts at conversation that would make even a native speaker weep. We had a "French Friday" where we were supposed to bring in French snacks. I thought I'd impress everyone by making crepes. Turns out, making crepes is a lot harder than it looks. I ended up with a kitchen that looked like a flour bomb exploded, and crepes that resembled sad, lumpy pancakes. The only thing French about them was the fact that I was too embarrassed to serve them to anyone.

Then there was the time we decided to watch a French film. I thought it would be a romantic comedy, you know, something light and fluffy. Instead, we ended up with a three-hour existential drama about a man who spends his life contemplating the meaning of existence while sitting in a café. By the end, we were all just as confused as the protagonist, wondering if we were supposed to laugh or cry. Spoiler alert: we did both.

And let's not forget the time we tried to learn a French song. We chose "La Vie en Rose," thinking it would be a beautiful addition to our repertoire. What we didn't realize was that singing in French is like trying to solve a Rubik's Cube while riding a unicycle. Half of us were belting out the wrong lyrics, while the other half were just making random sounds that vaguely resembled French. It was a cacophony that could only be described as "musical chaos."

By the end of the semester, I hadn't become fluent in French, but I had learned a few important lessons: namely, that it's okay to be a little ridiculous, that laughter can bridge any language barrier, and that sometimes, the best memories come from making a complete fool of yourself. So, here's to the French club, where the only thing we truly mastered was the art of having fun, one awkward mispronunciation at a time.

https://app.videogen.io/view/dsejai

Welcome To Junction City, Kansas, World Traveler

So, hosting a foreign exchange student. Let's just say it's like adopting a pet but with a lot more paperwork and fewer belly rubs. You think you're getting a cute little puppy, but instead, you end up with a full-grown kangaroo that doesn't speak your language and insists on hopping around your living room at 2 AM.

We were so excited when we found out we would be hosting a student from Germany. I imagined all the wonderful things we'd do together: cultural exchanges, cooking traditional meals, and bonding over our shared love for awkward family dinners. What I didn't anticipate was that our exchange student, let's call him Hans, would come equipped with a suitcase full of quirks and a penchant for mischief that could rival a toddler on a sugar high.

The first night, I tried to make a nice welcome dinner. I thought, "Let's impress him with some classic American cuisine!" So, I whipped up a feast of hamburgers and fries. I mean, who doesn't love a good burger? But Hans took one look at my culinary masterpiece and said, "In Germany, we have a saying: 'A hamburger is not a real meal.'" I was taken aback. I thought, "What do you mean? Are you going to pull out a schnitzel right now and start a food fight?"

As it turns out, Hans had a very different idea of what constitutes a meal. The next day, he decided to introduce me to the wonders of German cuisine. I was excited until I realized that his idea of cooking involved a lot of pickled things. I mean, I love a good pickle, but when your entire meal is just various forms of pickled vegetables, you start to question your life choices. I sat there, staring at a plate of pickled herring, thinking, "I never thought I'd be negotiating with a fish for my dinner."

Then there was the language barrier. Oh, the language barrier. Hans spoke English well enough, but there were moments when I felt like I needed a translator just to understand his jokes. One night, he told me a joke about a snail. I thought it was going to be a cute little pun, but it turned into a long, drawn-out story about a snail that wanted to ride a turtle. By the time he got to the punchline, I had forgotten what the joke was even about. I just sat there, nodding along, hoping my face didn't betray my confusion.

School was another adventure. I remember the first day he went to high school here. I thought it would be a great bonding experience to drive him. As we pulled into the parking lot, he looked at me with wide eyes and said, "Where are all the bicycles?" I laughed, thinking he was joking. But no, he was serious. Apparently, in Germany, students ride their bikes to school like it's an Olympic sport. Meanwhile, here in America, we drive our SUVs like we're training for the next NASCAR event.

After a week, Hans had made friends, and I was thrilled. I thought, "Finally, he'll have someone to talk to, and I can stop pretending to understand his snail jokes." But then he started bringing them over. Suddenly, our living room became a hangout for a group of teenagers who seemed to communicate in a language of memes and TikTok dances. I felt like I was hosting a foreign exchange student and his entire entourage.

But despite the chaos, I wouldn't trade the experience for anything. Sure, there were moments where I questioned my sanity, like when Hans tried to teach me the German version of "Twinkle, Twinkle, Little Star," which sounded more like a battle cry. Yet, through the laughter and the confusion, we became a family. I learned that hosting a foreign exchange student is less about the cultural exchange and more about the unexpected friendships that come from sharing a home, a few pickles, and a whole lot of laughter.

https://app.videogen.io/view/vsoyyt

A First Time For Everything, But With Pizza

High school first dates are like trying to navigate a minefield while blindfolded, with a marching band playing in the background. You think you know what you're doing, but really, you're just hoping you don't step on something that will blow up in your face. I remember my first date vividly, like a slow-motion train wreck that I couldn't look away from.

It all started with a note, because texting wasn't cool yet. I had this huge crush on Jenna from biology class. She had the kind of smile that could brighten up a rainy day and the laugh that made you feel like you were in on the world's best inside joke. So, naturally, I decided to write her a note. You know, the classic "Do you like me? Check yes or no." Romantic, right? Except, I accidentally wrote "Do you like me? Check yes or maybe." Maybe? What was I thinking? That's like giving her a loophole to say, "Well, I don't dislike you, but I'm not exactly sending you love letters either."

I somehow managed to get the note to her without losing a limb in the process. I was sweating bullets, convinced that the entire school was watching me. I could practically hear the theme music from a horror movie playing in my head. But shockingly, she said yes! I mean, she checked "yes" AND "maybe," but I was too busy doing a happy dance in my head to care about the "maybe" part.

So, we decided to go to the local pizza place after school. I had this grand idea that I would be the perfect gentleman. I would open the door for her, pull out her chair, and make her laugh so hard she'd forget her own name. But here's the thing—none of that happened. I was so nervous that I forgot how to walk. I tripped over my own feet right after I said, "I'll get the door!" I knocked into the glass, which made a sound like a gunshot in the quiet afternoon. Jenna laughed, and I turned fifty shades of red.

Inside the pizza place, I tried to play it cool, but I was sweating like a snowman in July. I ordered a pepperoni pizza, thinking it was a safe choice. But then I remembered I had a weird aversion to cheese. Why did I order pizza? What was I thinking? I had to pretend to enjoy every cheesy bite while silently praying I wouldn't end up in a dairy-induced coma.

We talked about school, music, and somehow ended up discussing the merits of pineapple on pizza. I was trying to sound sophisticated, like I had an opinion on culinary arts. "I mean, pineapple is a tropical fruit, so it's basically a vacation on a pizza." Who says that? I was one awkward metaphor away from being voted "Most Likely to Trip Over His Own Words."

Then, disaster struck. I took a big bite of pizza, and of course, the cheese decided to perform its own escape act. It stretched out like a rubber band, and before I knew it, I had cheese dangling from my chin like a bizarre piece of jewelry. Jenna's eyes widened as she tried to suppress her laughter. I could feel the heat rising in my cheeks, and I thought, "This is it. This is how I become a legend at school."

I wiped my chin, but instead of cleaning up, I just smeared sauce across my face like a war paint. "I'm just trying to be a pizza artist," I said, trying to salvage my dignity. Jenna laughed so hard she nearly choked on her soda. At that moment, I realized that maybe, just maybe, being a complete disaster wasn't the worst thing in the world.

By the end of the date, I was no longer worried about impressing her. I was just grateful she found my awkwardness endearing. We walked out of that pizza place, and I knew I had survived my first date.

Sure, I was covered in cheese and sauce, but I had made her laugh. And honestly, that's what made it all worth it.

https://app.videogen.io/view/wognbi

The Great Time Capsule Debate

Ah, the high school time capsule. That magical box where we're supposed to capture the essence of our teenage years, like some kind of archaeological artifact destined for future generations. I mean, who wouldn't want to dig up a box of our most embarrassing moments a few decades later? "Look, kids! Here's a pair of my old jeans! They were so tight, I couldn't breathe, but hey, it was 2005, and low rise was all the rage!"

The idea of a time capsule is both thrilling and terrifying. I remember the day our history teacher announced it. She stood there, all wide-eyed and enthusiastic, like she had just discovered fire or something. "Let's create a time capsule!" she exclaimed, as if we were all going to be the next Indiana Jones, digging through the dirt to uncover our teenage treasures. I could see the gears turning in my classmates' heads. Some were picturing their favorite snacks, others their beloved cell phones, and a few were probably considering how to sneak in a few embarrassing photos of their crushes.

And then came the brainstorming session. Oh, the brainstorming session. It was like a chaotic episode of "Shark Tank," but instead of million-dollar ideas, we were pitching our most ridiculous thoughts. "How about we put in a mixtape of our favorite songs?" someone suggested. A mixtape? In a world of Spotify playlists and Apple Music? I could already see future generations scratching their heads, wondering why we thought "Bye Bye Bye" was an anthem of our existence. "What's a mixtape?" they'd ask, and I'd just smile knowingly, like a wise old sage who had seen things.

Then there was the inevitable debate over what to include. I mean, how do you encapsulate four years of awkwardness, angst, and questionable fashion choices into a single box? "Let's throw in a yearbook!" one classmate shouted. Brilliant, except that our yearbook was basically a glorified collection of selfies and inside jokes that would make absolutely no sense to anyone outside our little bubble. "Remember that time we thought it was a good idea to get matching haircuts?" I could hear future students laughing at our poor decisions.

As the days passed, the excitement morphed into panic. What if we didn't include the right things? What if future generations thought we were boring? I mean, we had TikTok and Instagram, but what would they think if we just tossed in a few crumpled notes and a half-eaten bag of Flamin' Hot Cheetos? "Look, kids! This is what we used to snack on while we binge-watched reality TV!"

The pressure mounted as we approached the deadline. I found myself wandering the aisles of Target, contemplating the significance of a rubber duck. "Is this quirky enough? Will it represent my high school experience?" I ended up buying a stress ball shaped like a brain. "Perfect! This symbolizes how I felt during finals week!"

Finally, the day arrived. We gathered around the box, each of us clutching our contributions like they were golden tickets to the chocolate factory. I tossed in my stress ball, and someone else added a pair of socks with pizza slices on them because, apparently, that was a thing we all loved. We sealed the box, our laughter echoing in the air, and buried it in a corner of the school yard.

As I walked away, I felt a strange mix of nostalgia and relief. We had captured our high school experience, or at least a bizarre snapshot of it. Who knows what future kids will think when they unearth our time capsule? Maybe they'll laugh, maybe they'll cringe, but one thing's for sure: they'll definitely be grateful they don't have to wear low-rise jeans.

https://app.videogen.io/view/ianuvh

Study All Night, Test And Forget It All

I remember the night vividly, the kind of night that feels like it could only exist in the pages of a coming-of-age novel, or maybe a sitcom that never quite made it past the pilot episode. It was the night of the big chemistry exam, and there I was, armed with nothing but a half-eaten bag of stale potato chips, a bottle of lukewarm soda, and a textbook that had seen better days—like the days when I actually opened it. My friends and I had decided to embark on this all-night study marathon, a noble quest for knowledge that quickly devolved into chaos, laughter, and a questionable amount of caffeinated beverages.

We gathered at my friend Jake's house, the designated study headquarters, which was really just a glorified den of teenage procrastination. The living room was strewn with textbooks, highlighters, and enough snack wrappers to create a small landfill. It was like a war zone, but instead of soldiers, we had a ragtag team of sleep-deprived high schoolers, all armed with the latest in study technology: a smartphone with unlimited data and a YouTube playlist dedicated to lo-fi beats. Who needs a study guide when you can have a soothing soundtrack of elevator music?

As the clock ticked past midnight, we realized that we hadn't actually studied anything. Instead, we had spent the last hour debating the merits of various pizza toppings and whether pineapple belonged on pizza. Spoiler alert: it does not, according to the unanimous vote of three out of four sleep-deprived teenagers. I mean, who has time for chemistry when you can have a heated discussion about food? It was like a culinary summit, only instead of world leaders, we had a group of teenagers who couldn't even agree on what constitutes a proper breakfast.

Around two a.m., the caffeine kicked in, and with it came the realization that we were in way over our heads. I looked at my friend Sarah, who was trying to make sense of the periodic table while simultaneously scrolling through TikTok. "Sarah, are you studying or just watching people dance?" I asked, half-joking. She looked up, wide-eyed, and said, "Why not both?" That's when I knew we were doomed. We were like a bunch of squirrels trying to solve a Rubik's Cube—completely lost and slightly manic.

By three a.m., the snacks had turned from a source of fuel to a source of regret. I took a long sip of my soda and immediately regretted it. My stomach felt like a science experiment gone wrong, bubbling and churning like a volatile chemical reaction. I glanced over at Jake, who was sprawled out on the couch, snoring loudly. His textbook was open on his chest, and I could practically hear the pages mocking him. "You think you can just sleep through this, huh?" I whispered, but he didn't hear me. He was probably dreaming about the periodic table, or maybe just dreaming about pizza—who knows?

As the sun began to rise, we made a last-ditch effort to cram. I flipped through my notes, hoping to absorb the information through sheer willpower. "Okay, what's the atomic number of carbon?" I asked, looking around for any semblance of a response. Silence. "Anyone? Bueller? Bueller?" I joked, but the only answer was the sound of crickets—literal crickets, because Jake had left the window open and now we had an infestation.

Finally, as dawn broke and the first rays of sunlight streamed through the window, we surrendered to our fate. We had learned nothing, but we had bonded over our shared misery. We stumbled into school that day, bleary-eyed and clutching our coffee cups like lifelines. As we sat down for the exam, I couldn't help but think that the real lesson of the night wasn't about chemistry at all; it was about friendship, resilience, and the undeniable truth that sometimes, laughter is the best study aid.

https://app.videogen.io/view/qigwml

Cracking The Top Ten, One Crip Course At A Time

I remember the first time I saw the academic top ten list at my high school. It was like stumbling upon the Holy Grail, except instead of a shiny cup, it was a piece of paper taped to the wall, filled with names that seemed to glow with an otherworldly light. I stood there, staring at it, my heart racing. It was as if I had discovered the secret to life itself, and there it was, just a few grades away. I wanted my name on that list so badly I could almost taste it. Spoiler alert: I never made it.

The first step in my quest was to devise a strategy. I approached it like a military operation. I had my notebooks, my highlighters, and an arsenal of caffeine in the form of energy drinks that I convinced myself were "brain fuel." I even created a color-coded calendar that would make a kindergarten teacher weep with envy. I was ready. Or so I thought.

The first thing I learned was that high school is a competitive jungle. It's like Survivor, but instead of being voted off the island, you get a B- in Chemistry. My first challenge came in the form of a pop quiz. I walked into class, blissfully unaware that my teacher had decided to test our knowledge of the periodic table. I had studied everything but the periodic table. I mean, who needs to know that hydrogen is H and oxygen is O? I thought I was going to ace the quiz on Shakespeare! Spoiler alert: I didn't.

Then there was the infamous group project. I teamed up with the overachievers, the ones who could recite the entire textbook from memory. They were great, but they also had this strange ability to make me feel like I was dragging a boulder uphill while they floated effortlessly beside me. I did my best to contribute, but it turns out my idea of "teamwork" was mostly Googling facts and pretending I was a valuable member of the group. When we presented, they dazzled the teacher with their charisma while I stood awkwardly in the back, nodding like a bobblehead.

As the semester wore on, I realized that my social life was disappearing faster than my chances of making that top ten list. I was spending more time with my textbooks than with my friends. My weekends turned into marathons of studying, punctuated only by brief, panicked moments of existential dread. I would sit there, surrounded by a fortress of textbooks, wondering if I was sacrificing my youth for a piece of paper. But hey, at least I was going to be on that list! Right? Wrong.

Midterms rolled around, and I was convinced I would finally show my teachers what I was made of. I walked into the exam room, armed with a pencil and a prayer. The first question was a curveball, something about the economic implications of the War of 1812. I stared at it like it was written in ancient Greek. I had studied the War of 1812, but apparently, I had missed the memo about the economic implications. I scribbled down something that resembled an answer, but I was pretty sure it was more like a haiku than an economic analysis.

After the grades came back, I found myself in a familiar spot: just outside the top ten. I was like a contestant on a game show who had just missed the final round. "Thank you for playing! Here's your consolation prize: a lifetime of mediocre grades!"

By the end of the year, I had come to terms with my fate. I didn't make the top ten list, and you know what? It was okay. I learned that there's more to high school than grades. I discovered the joy of spontaneous pizza parties, late-night study sessions that devolved into gossip fests, and the realization that sometimes, the best memories are made outside of the classroom. So, I may not have made it to the top ten, but I did learn how to make a mean pizza roll, and honestly, that's a skill I can take into adulthood.

https://app.videogen.io/view/yeioei

My Fellow High School Americans

You know, when I decided to run for class president, I thought it would be a simple enough endeavor. I mean, how hard could it be? Just a few speeches, a couple of posters, maybe some free snacks to lure in voters? I had it all mapped out in my head. I was going to be the hero of the hallways, the champion of cafeteria lunches, the savior of study hall! Little did I know, I was stepping into a whirlwind of chaos that would make a reality TV show look like a Sunday picnic.

First off, let's talk about the campaign strategy. I figured I'd go the traditional route—posters, speeches, and maybe a catchy slogan. So there I was, standing in front of my bedroom wall, armed with a roll of colorful paper and a pack of markers, ready to unleash my creativity. After an hour of intense brainstorming, I came up with my slogan: "Vote for Me, I'm Not a Jerk!" It was perfect, right? I mean, who wouldn't want to vote for the non-jerk? But then I thought, what if everyone else was also running on the "not a jerk" platform? I could just see it: "Vote for Me, I'm Not a Jerk, Either!" Suddenly, I was in a high school election that sounded more like a kindergarten playground argument.

Then came the speeches. I practiced in front of my mirror, channeling my inner politician. I imagined the crowd hanging on my every word, cheering me on like I was about to solve world hunger. But when the day finally arrived, my heart was racing faster than a squirrel on espresso. I stood up there, staring at my classmates, who were more interested in their phones than my grand vision for the school. I tried to make eye contact, but all I saw were the tops of heads and the occasional yawn. I mean, who knew that "free pizza" had more allure than "a better school experience"?

And let's not forget the debate. Oh, the debate! It was supposed to be a serious affair, but it turned into a roast session. My opponent, who I swear was born with a microphone in his hand, started throwing around accusations like confetti. "You're just a puppet!" he yelled, and I was like, "A puppet? Have you seen my dance moves?" I couldn't help but laugh. I mean, if I'm a puppet, then he's a marionette tangled in strings! But instead of clapping, the crowd just looked confused. Apparently, high schoolers don't appreciate clever metaphors when they're busy scrolling through TikTok.

Then came the campaign trail. I thought I'd charm my way into voters' hearts by shaking hands and kissing babies—except, you know, the babies were actually just my friends who were too busy trying to dodge my campaign. I made the mistake of setting up a booth at lunch, thinking it would be a great way to connect. Instead, I ended up as the designated snack distributor. "Vote for me, and you get free cookies!" I shouted, and suddenly, I was less of a candidate and more of a cookie dealer. I even had a friend come up to me and say, "I don't care who wins, just keep the cookies coming."

As the election day loomed closer, I realized that all my grand plans were slowly unraveling. I was just a kid trying to navigate the murky waters of high school politics, where popularity was king and logic was nowhere to be found. But you know what? I learned something valuable through all this chaos. Whether I won or lost, I was brave enough to put myself out there, to stand up and say, "Hey, I care!" And honestly, if I can survive a high school election, I can probably handle anything life throws at me—except maybe a math test. That's a whole different kind of nightmare.

https://app.videogen.io/view/bhnyhd

Pep Rally Fever: Catch It? I Mean, CATCH IT!!

You know, I've been thinking a lot about pep rallies lately. It's that time of year again, when the entire high school gathers in the gym, and I can't help but wonder: who decided that a bunch of teenagers, fueled by questionable snacks and the awkwardness of adolescence, would make a good audience for a pep rally? I mean, really, if you want to see a bunch of kids who look like they'd rather be anywhere else, just walk into a pep rally.

First off, let's talk about the noise. The moment you step into that gym, it's like you've walked into a concert for a band that no one wants to see. The cheerleaders are doing their best to whip up enthusiasm, but let's face it, half the kids are just trying to figure out how to avoid eye contact with their crush. I swear, there's an unwritten rule that says if you're wearing a school spirit shirt, you must also be equipped with a side-eye for anyone who dares to look at you. The only thing louder than the cheers is the sound of sneakers squeaking against the polished floor as everyone shuffles around, trying to find a seat that doesn't come with a view of their ex.

And then there are the speeches. Oh, the speeches. You know, the ones where the principal gets up and tries to rally the troops like he's leading a battalion into battle. "Let's show our school spirit!" he says, and you can practically hear the collective groan from the back row. Seriously, Mr. Johnson, we're not storming the beaches of Normandy; we're just trying to survive geometry class. But he's undeterred, waving his arms like a conductor trying to orchestrate a symphony of apathy.

The student body president steps up next, probably the only person in the room who genuinely believes that this pep rally is the highlight of the school year. She's got that bright smile and a voice that could shatter glass. "We're going to win the championship!" she declares, and I can't help but wonder if she's checked the score of the last game. I mean, we're talking about a team that hasn't won since the invention of sliced bread. But hey, who needs facts when you have enthusiasm?

And then there are the games. Oh, the games. They always pick the most ridiculous contests, like tug-of-war or a relay race that involves balancing a spoon on your nose. I'm not sure how this is supposed to build school spirit, but it does provide some excellent entertainment. Watching the jocks try to run while balancing a spoon is like watching a nature documentary on a bunch of confused gazelles. You can practically hear the narrator's voice: "And here we see the alpha male, unsure of how to navigate this strange terrain."

And let's not forget the snacks. There's always a table laden with chips, popcorn, and those tiny cups of fruit that are somehow both a healthy option and a sad reminder of how your parents packed your lunch. You grab a handful of chips, and suddenly you're a part of a social experiment to see how many teenagers can fit into a single corner of the gym without actually interacting with one another. It's like a game of human Tetris, where the goal is to avoid any physical contact while still managing to snag a cupcake.

By the end of the pep rally, you leave feeling a mix of confusion and mild amusement. You've cheered for a team you barely care about, listened to speeches that could put a caffeinated squirrel to sleep, and laughed at the awkwardness of it all. As you walk out, you can't help but think: maybe, just maybe, the real spirit of the pep rally isn't about winning games or school pride. It's about surviving the chaos, armed with nothing but a bag of chips and a sense of humor. And honestly, isn't that what high school is all about?

https://app.videogen.io/view/vnadix

The Proof Is In The Senior Picture

So, let's talk about high school senior pictures. You know, those iconic snapshots that are supposed to capture the essence of your teenage self, the one that your parents will hang on the wall for eternity, right next to the family portrait where everyone's smiling awkwardly in matching sweaters. I remember the day of my senior picture like it was yesterday, a glorious mix of excitement and dread, and a hint of existential crisis.

First off, there's the outfit dilemma. You'd think I was preparing for the Met Gala rather than a simple photo shoot. I mean, what does one wear to encapsulate four years of high school experience? I spent hours rifling through my closet, tossing clothes onto my bed like I was auditioning for a reality show about fashion disasters. Should I go for the classic "I'm a serious scholar" look with a blazer and a button-up? Or maybe the "I'm a free spirit" vibe with a flowy dress and a flower crown? Spoiler alert: I ended up in a shirt that was a little too tight and jeans that were definitely too loose, because that's how high school works—confusion at its finest.

Then there's the hair. Oh, the hair. I had a plan, of course. I wanted those beachy waves that look effortless, like I just rolled out of bed looking fabulous. Instead, I ended up with a frizzy mess that could have been mistaken for a small animal. I tried to tame it with every product known to humankind: mousse, gel, hairspray, you name it. I was practically a chemistry experiment gone wrong. My mom walked in and said, "Are you sure you don't want to just wear a hat?" I mean, thanks, Mom, but that's not exactly the look I was going for.

And let's not forget about the makeup. I decided to go for a "natural" look, which in my case meant slathering on enough foundation to create a new layer of skin. I was convinced that I needed to cover every blemish, every imperfection, until I looked in the mirror and realized I resembled a slightly less scary version of a porcelain doll. My eyeshadow was a bold choice, too; I thought I was channeling a glamorous influencer, but really, I looked like I was preparing for a clown audition.

Finally, the moment arrived. I walked into the studio, and the photographer greeted me with a smile that said, "I've seen it all." He adjusted his camera and asked me to strike a pose. A pose? What do you mean, a pose? I froze like a deer in headlights, trying to remember what I'd practiced in the mirror. Should I smile with my teeth or go for the mysterious smirk? In the end, I settled for a grin that looked like I was trying to hold in a sneeze.

As the session progressed, I realized that I had no idea what I was doing. The photographer kept saying things like, "Give me more energy!" and "Channel your inner model!" My inner model was currently hiding under a pile of self-doubt, so I just flailed around, trying to look casual while simultaneously feeling like I was auditioning for a role in a really bad sitcom.

After what felt like a lifetime, the session finally ended, and I walked out feeling like I had just survived a marathon. I was exhausted, my hair was a disaster, and I had a strange feeling that I'd just captured the most awkward moments of my teenage life in a single frame.

Fast forward a few weeks, and the proofs arrived. I opened the envelope, and there it was: my senior picture. I stared at it, trying to decipher if I looked more like a high school senior or a confused raccoon. In the end, I realized it didn't matter. It was a snapshot of a moment in time, a reminder of the chaos, the laughter, and the sheer absurdity of being a teenager. And honestly, if I can survive that, I can survive anything.

https://app.videogen.io/view/lsavel

Spirit Week Shenanigans

Ah, Spirit Week, that glorious time of year when high school students rally together to show their school pride in the most extravagant and often ridiculous ways possible. It's like a week-long carnival, but instead of cotton candy and ferris wheels, you get awkward outfits and the lingering smell of desperation. I remember my own Spirit Week vividly, a kaleidoscope of questionable fashion choices and a relentless quest for popularity that, in hindsight, was utterly absurd.

The week kicked off with "Pajama Day." Now, you might think, "Oh, how cozy! I can roll out of bed and still look stylish!" But let me tell you, nothing says "I'm ready to learn" like a pair of plaid flannel pants that are two sizes too big and a T-shirt featuring a cartoon cat that says, "I woke up like this." The hallways were a sea of mismatched socks and bedhead hairstyles, and I, in my infinite wisdom, decided that a full onesie was the way to go. Picture this: a bright yellow duck onesie, complete with a beak that flopped around as I walked. I was the embodiment of "I give up." But hey, at least I was warm, right?

Then came "Twin Day," where you had to find a partner and coordinate outfits. My best friend and I, in a fit of creativity, decided to dress as a pair of bananas. Yes, actual bananas. We spent hours crafting our costumes, complete with yellow shirts, green hats, and a whole lot of duct tape. We strutted down the hallway, ready to peel away the competition, when we were met with a chorus of laughter. "Look at the bananas!" they shouted. And you know what? I didn't even care. We were the fruit of the week, and I'd take that title any day.

Midweek rolled around, and it was "Decade Day." I thought I was being clever by channeling the 80s with my neon leg warmers and oversized hair. I was ready to dance my way through the day, but the reality was far less glamorous. I walked into school, and suddenly, I felt like I had time-traveled to a bad music video. I was met with a barrage of confused stares and whispers. "Is she serious?" "What even is that?" I tried to embody the spirit of the decade, but instead, I became the punchline of every joke in the cafeteria.

Next up was "Color Wars," where each grade was assigned a color, and you had to deck yourself out from head to toe. Freshmen were red, sophomores were blue, juniors were green, and seniors were, of course, black, because nothing screams "I'm almost done with high school" like a funeral for your youth. I went all out, wearing a bright green tutu, face paint, and a headband with floppy ears. I looked like a demented leprechaun, and the worst part? We lost. I was devastated. I had put my heart and soul into that tutu, and now, I was the laughingstock of the school.

Finally, Friday arrived, the grand finale: "School Spirit Day." I thought I could redeem myself by donning my school colors, a T-shirt that was two sizes too small, and a massive foam finger that I could barely lift. I was ready to cheer my classmates on, but all I could think about was how uncomfortable I was. I felt like a walking advertisement for the school, and frankly, I was tired. Tired of the costumes, the pressure, and the constant need to prove my spirit.

In retrospect, Spirit Week was a whirlwind of laughter, embarrassment, and a whole lot of ridiculousness. It taught me that sometimes, it's not about winning or losing but about the memories you create and the friends you make along the way—even if those memories involve a duck onesie and a banana costume. So here's to Spirit Week, the ultimate test of creativity, friendship, and the willingness to look utterly foolish for the sake of school pride.

https://app.videogen.io/view/lgysxm

Away Games: A Faint Hint Of Sulfur In The Air

You ever been to an away football game against your school's biggest rival? It's like stepping into a gladiatorial arena, but with more face paint and less actual fighting. The tension in the air is thicker than the nacho cheese at the concession stand. You arrive, and it's like entering a foreign country. The rival school is decked out in their colors, which are somehow both obnoxious and oddly mesmerizing, like a neon sign that's been left on too long. You can practically hear the collective heartbeat of their student section, and it's pounding with the rhythm of "We're better than you!" chants.

As we pull into the parking lot, I'm already regretting my decision to wear our school's colors. I mean, I love my school, but you'd think I was wearing a bullseye on my back. I'm practically begging the universe not to encounter any of their fans. Then there's the moment when you step out of the car, and it hits you: the smell of hot dogs, the sound of a marching band practicing a song you've heard a million times, and the palpable energy of a crowd that's ready to explode at the slightest provocation. It's exhilarating and terrifying all at once.

You walk into the stadium, and it's like entering a different dimension. The rival students are all wearing matching jerseys, and they've even coordinated their haircuts. I swear, if I see one more kid with a perfectly coiffed mullet, I might just lose it. They've got their faces painted in a way that looks like they were attacked by a paintball gun, and they're all holding signs that say things like "Our Team is Better" and "Your School Sucks." Very subtle, guys. Very original.

I'm trying to keep my cool, but my heart is racing. The game kicks off, and the energy is electric. Every time their team scores, the crowd erupts into a cacophony of cheers and chants, while we're over in our corner, trying to muster up the courage to cheer for our team without sounding like a dying cat. And let me tell you, the rivalry runs deep. It's like a soap opera out there, with all the drama and none of the commercial breaks.

Then there's the halftime show, which is basically a theatrical production designed to humiliate the opposing team. The rival band comes out, and they're marching in formation, playing a song that's somehow both catchy and infuriating. It's like they're taunting us, and I can feel the collective groan of our side. Meanwhile, our band is over there trying to keep up, but it's like watching a toddler trying to dance to a beat they can't hear.

As the game progresses, the tension mounts. It's like a rollercoaster ride, with all the ups and downs of a plot twist you didn't see coming. Our team scores, and for a brief moment, we're on top of the world. But then the rival team retaliates, and it's like we've been punched in the gut. The cheers from their side are deafening, and I swear I can see the smugness radiating off their fans like heat waves.

By the end of the game, I'm emotionally spent. I've laughed, I've cried, and I've almost thrown a nacho at a rival fan who wouldn't stop shouting about how much better they are. Spoiler alert: they won the game. But honestly, it doesn't even matter. The real victory is in the shared experience, the camaraderie of being with friends, and the ridiculousness of it all.

As we file out of the stadium, I realize that even though we lost, we're still a part of something bigger. Rivalries are what make high school sports memorable. It's not just about the score; it's about the stories we'll tell, the laughter we'll share, and the ridiculousness of it all. And maybe, just maybe, I'll be back next year, ready to face the neon warriors once again.

https://app.videogen.io/view/quenbh

Reflections Of A Valedictorian

So, here I am, the high school valedictorian, standing on the precipice of my teenage dreams, and I can't help but think, "Wow, how did I get here?" It's not like I was the kid who had it all figured out. I wasn't the star athlete, the popular kid, or even the one with a killer TikTok account. No, I was more like the kid who spent lunch in the library, surrounded by books and the faint smell of old paper, contemplating the meaning of life while trying to figure out how to ask someone to prom. Spoiler alert: I never did.

Becoming valedictorian is a bit like winning the lottery, except instead of cash, you get a diploma and the responsibility of giving a speech that people will likely forget before they even leave the auditorium. But hey, at least I get to wear this ridiculous gown that looks like it was designed by someone who had a very specific vision of what a potato should wear. And don't even get me started on the cap. I mean, who decided that we should all wear hats that resemble a flying saucer? I half expect aliens to land and abduct us right after the ceremony. "Congratulations, Earthlings! You're now all valedictorians of the intergalactic school of mediocrity!"

The pressure to succeed was real. My parents had this idea that being valedictorian was the golden ticket to success. They'd say things like, "You know, if you study hard and get good grades, you can get into any college you want!" And I believed them. I mean, who wouldn't? So there I was, nose deep in textbooks, cramming for exams, and listening to motivational podcasts at 2 a.m., while my friends were out living their best lives, posting about parties and adventures. I was the kid who got excited about a new edition of the encyclopedia. "Did you see the new volume? It has a whole section on the history of cheese!" Because, you know, cheese is important.

And then there were the late nights, fueled by caffeine and a desperate need to prove myself. I became a master of the art of procrastination. I could write a ten-page research paper in one night, but only if I had a deadline looming over me like a dark cloud. "What's that? The paper is due tomorrow? Time to channel my inner Shakespeare!" Meanwhile, my friends were like, "Hey, want to binge-watch the latest season of that show?" And I'd be like, "I can't! I have to study!" As if Netflix was the ultimate villain in my quest for academic glory.

But let's not forget the teachers. Oh, the teachers. They were like my personal cheerleading squad, but with less pom-poms and more red pens. I remember one teacher saying, "You have so much potential! You could be anything you want!" And I thought, "Great, but can I be a professional napper? Because that's my true calling." Instead, I was stuck balancing calculus equations and Shakespearean sonnets, all while trying to figure out how to manage my social life, which was basically nonexistent.

And now, as I stand here, ready to deliver my valedictorian speech, I realize that I have no idea what to say. Should I inspire my classmates with tales of perseverance and hard work? Or should I just tell them that it's okay to not have it all figured out? Because let's be honest, most of us are just winging it. We're all just a bunch of kids trying to navigate this crazy thing called life, armed with nothing but our dreams, a questionable amount of caffeine, and the hope that we don't trip on stage while accepting our diplomas.

So, here's to us, the class of whatever year this is. We made it! And if life doesn't go according to plan, at least we can always look back and say we were valedictorians. That's something, right? Now, if only I could figure out how to turn that into a career...

https://app.videogen.io/view/xxjblu

https://app.videogen.io/view/xxjblu

I'm 18: You Can't (Or Can) Tell Me What To Do

Turning 18 in high school is like being handed a shiny new toy that you're not quite sure how to play with. I mean, one minute you're the kid who can't even buy a pack of gum without parental supervision, and the next minute, you're thrust into this wild adult world where you can vote, sign contracts, and—get this—buy lottery tickets! It's like they looked at us and said, "Congratulations! You're now legally responsible for your own bad decisions!"

Let's be real for a second. Who thought it was a good idea to let teenagers with raging hormones and questionable decision-making skills suddenly become adults? I remember sitting in my last high school class, staring at the clock, counting down the minutes until I was officially a legal adult. I felt like I was in some bizarre countdown to a space launch. "Three... two... one... Happy adulthood! You can now make all the mistakes you want without anyone being able to stop you!"

And then there's the whole "you can vote" thing. I mean, I can barely decide what to have for lunch, and now I'm supposed to choose the next leader of the free world? I remember thinking, "Do I even know what a senator does? Is that the person who fixes your car or the one who makes sure the school lunch is edible?" Not to mention the pressure of registering to vote. I felt like I was signing my life away, like I was committing to a lifetime of political arguments at family gatherings. "Oh great, now I can't just roll my eyes when Uncle Bob starts ranting about taxes. I have to engage! What if I accidentally agree with him?"

And let's talk about the parties. Turning 18 means you're suddenly invited to all these "adult" parties where everyone insists that you should drink because, hey, you're an adult now! I went to my first party after turning 18, and it was like entering a different dimension. There I was, surrounded by people who had clearly been drinking since they were 15, and I'm just standing there with my sparkling water, feeling like a toddler at a grown-up dinner party. Everyone was shouting, "Let's celebrate your freedom!" while I was just trying to figure out how to navigate this new social landscape. I thought, "Is it too late to go back to being 17? I can't even keep up with the conversation! What does 'adulting' even mean?"

Then there's the added pressure of adulthood. Suddenly, everyone expects you to have your life figured out. "What are your plans after high school?" they ask, as if I've been secretly plotting my career path since kindergarten. I'm still trying to figure out how to do my own laundry without turning everything pink! I mean, I can barely keep my room clean, and now I'm supposed to be a responsible adult? The only thing I'm responsible for is making sure I don't accidentally set my microwave on fire when I'm reheating leftover pizza.

And let's not forget the joy of adult responsibilities. I got my first credit card, and I felt like I was holding a golden ticket. But no one warned me about the fine print! I thought I was rich until I realized I had to pay it back. I'm standing there at the store, thinking, "Wow, I can buy this fancy new gadget! Oh wait, I'll be paying for it until I'm 30. Great."

So, here I am, 18, navigating this chaotic world of adulthood while still trying to figure out if I should be studying for finals or binge-watching my favorite show. It's a wild ride, and I'm just trying to keep my head above water. But hey, at least I can finally sign my own permission slips! That's got to count for something, right?

https://app.videogen.io/view/xpyjcl

Also by Kevin Lawson

Drawn But Not Forgotten
The First Time I Ever...
The REAL College Survival Guide
The REAL High School Survival Guide